THE
(FAIRLY)
MAGIC SHOW

AND OTHER STORIES

ROB KEELEY

Matador
9 Priory Business Park,
Wistow Road, Kibworth Beauchamp,
Leicestershire. LE8 0RX
Tel: (+44) 116 279 2299
Fax: (+44) 116 279 2277
Email: books@troubador.co.uk
Web: www.troubador.co.uk/matador

ISBN 978 1780883 014

British Library Cataloguing in Publication Data.
A catalogue record for this book is available from the British Library.

Typeset by Troubador Publishing Ltd, Leicester, UK

Matador is an imprint of Troubador Publishing Ltd

Printed and bound in the UK by TJ International, Padstow, Cornwall

Items should be returned on or before the last date shown below. Items not already requested by other borrowers may be renewed in person, in writing or by telephone. To renew, please quote the number on the barcode label. To renew online a PIN is required. This can be requested at your local library. Renew online @ **www.dublincitypubliclibraries.ie** Fines charged for overdue items will include postage incurred in recovery. Damage to or loss of items will be charged to the borrower.

Leabharlanna Poiblí Chathair Bhaile Átha Cliath
Dublin City Public Libraries

Baile Átha Cliath
Dublin City

Date Due	Date Due	Date Due

Contents

The (Fairly) Magic Show

"Happy Birthday, Molly!"

Molly smiled. She'd known that was coming. It was a family tradition, every birthday. Even after all these years, she still had to pretend to be surprised.

As soon as she walked into the kitchen for breakfast, there were Mum and Dad and Stuart, her big brother, surrounded by presents. And the candles on her cake were already lit, even though it was only eight o'clock in the morning.

Molly blew all the candles out with one gale-force blast of air, taking out a piece of toast at the same time.

She started to open her presents straight away. There was a mug from Uncle Pete. A soap-bag for her holidays from Nan and Grandpa. A baggy jumper from Auntie Kay. She really would have to have a word with Auntie Kay.

Mum and Dad's present was the best – a silver bracelet. Molly slipped it onto her wrist straight away.

And even Stuart had spent £1.50 on a bag of sweets.

There was one final parcel, a mystery one wrapped in dark green stripy paper.

"That's a little extra one from your Dad and me," Mum explained. She smiled. "Well. After Stuart's last show. You were saying you'd like to have a try."

Molly tore off the wrapping paper.

Inside was a big, black box covered in moons and stars.

And on the lid it said:

"MAGIC SET".

"Oh, no way?" Stuart had seen the lid too, and was looking annoyed. "Mum? You can't have *two* magicians, in the same family!"

He took a proud glance towards a framed photograph that stood on a nearby shelf. It showed Stuart, in his best black shirt and red bow-tie, with a white felt rabbit popping its head out of his top pocket. He was holding a cheap plastic trophy emblazoned with the legend: "Holiday Park Talent Trail".

"No reason why not," Dad said. "These things do run in families."

"I bet I can do it as well as you." Molly peered into the box.

There was a magic wand, and two decks of cards – one red-backed, the other blue. There was a magic handkerchief in red and blue, and a matchbox for making things disappear. There were three plastic thimbles, and four rings. There was a magic bottle in shiny blue plastic, and a small bunch of magic flowers.

"What're they gonna say at Magic Club?" Stuart turned his plea towards Dad.

"Maybe Molly could join?" Dad suggested.

"You're kidding me!" Stuart looked horror-stricken. "I've just started doing illusions! A flying dove and a levitating cube! And then *she* comes on and does the magic hanky!"

"I don't want to hear any more about it." Mum moved towards the cooker. "Molly's every bit as entitled to do magic tricks as you. There's nothing wrong with healthy competition."

She turned her attention to their breakfast. Dad moved to assist.

Stuart leaned over towards Molly.

Their eyes met.

"Get one thing clear," Stuart said. "*You* can't do magic. *I'm* the one who does magic round here. And everyone knows all the great magicians are men."

He reached across the tabletop and picked up the card that had been attached to Molly's parcel. It said: "To Molly. Happy magic-making! Love, Mum and Dad".

With a flick of Stuart's fingers, the card disappeared.

Stuart's eyes narrowed.

"May the best man win."

First thing after breakfast, Molly started to dip into the magic set.

She could just see herself, in a few years' time. Performing grand illusions, in London and Las Vegas. The hushed awe of audiences, the spotlights shining through the coloured smoke as she made her assistants disappear from the silver-fronted magic cabinet.

Half an hour later, she wasn't so sure. It wasn't quite as easy as she'd expected. You needed to be so clever, so deft with your fingers, to do all but the simplest tricks. Hiding something from the audience, even with the aid of a handkerchief or a magic box, was proving to be very difficult. And even shuffling cards was a problem. They'd been on the floor twice already.

She turned to see Stuart standing in the doorway.

"Having trouble?" He had two coins, one in each hand, and was making them disappear and reappear without even having to look. "Take my advice. Leave it to the professionals."

"I'm doing fine, thank you," Molly said.

"Go on, then," Stuart said. "Let's see."

Molly paused, just for a moment, before picking up the blue deck of cards.

"Pick one."

Stuart did so. He chose a card, looked at it, then pushed it back into the deck. Molly did her best to shuffle.

"Oh dear." Stuart grinned. He looked down at the carpet. "I hope my card's not down there."

Molly took a long and careful look through what was left of the deck, rather like a librarian checking a card index.

She produced a card.

"King of Spades?"

"No." Stuart smirked. "Ten of Hearts."

He flicked his fingers, and the missing card appeared in his hand.

"You see, that *wasn't* the card I put back. I only pretended to. I palmed my card, before you even started to look for it."

"That's not fair!" Molly cried.

"It's the sort of thing *professionals* do." Stuart moved casually to the coffee table, picking up Molly's plastic rings and thimbles. "A bit difficult for little kids, of course."

"You wait." Molly's face darkened. "All I need is practice. With a bit of practice, I'll be as good as you."

Then she said it.

"In fact, I'm going to do a magic show tonight. At my party. At Nan and Grandpa's."

Afterwards, Molly wondered whether she should have said that.

She didn't even look at her other presents, but spent all day with the magic set. She read all the instructions very carefully, and practised her small selection of tricks over and over again.

And slowly, she did start to get a little better. After dropping the cards five more times and tying herself in knots with the magic handkerchief, she started to become more confident, and to perform the effects more smoothly. By three o'clock she had mastered her first card trick.

But when the time arrived to go to Nan and Grandpa's, Molly still wasn't sure she was ready.

And she knew that Stuart would be watching her.

"I take the magic wand." Molly's voice sounded very high as she stood in the back room of Nan and Grandpa's house. "I hold it up in the air. I take my hands away. And look! The wand floats! In mid-air."

Nan and Grandpa and Mum and Dad smiled and clapped. But Molly could see Stuart smirking. She knew he could see the pencil up her sleeve that was holding the wand up.

Her magic show was going all right. But the matchbox was a bit small for a big audience. So were the tricks with the handkerchief. And she was still too clumsy to do a lot of the harder tricks.

"Nothing up my sleeve…" Stuart muttered.

"Stuart!" Mum gave him a look.

"And…" Molly brought the wand back to earth. She was quickly running out of patter. "And…er… it comes down again."

"Very good, Molly." Dad applauded.

The rest of the grown-ups followed. But their applause sounded polite. Molly could tell they weren't really impressed.

Stuart wasn't clapping at all.

Molly took a deep breath.

"Interval," she said firmly.

"You've got to help me!" Molly took Stuart to one side.

"Me?" Stuart smiled. "*You're* the magician."

"Oh, don't be mean!" Molly said. "Here's what we do."

She gave Stuart the magic flowers. Then she headed for the patio door.

"I'm going to draw the curtains over the door. You go

6

outside. Then, when I wave the wand, stick the flowers through the curtains and move them up and down."

"You're kidding!" Stuart said.

Then he smiled.

"All right. I'll do it."

Molly gave him a funny look.

Then she went back to the rest of the family.

"Act Two."

"I take the magic wand." Molly held the wand. "I wave it towards the door. And from the curtains, appears – a magnificent bouquet of flowers!"

Nothing happened. Molly tried again.

"A magnificent bouquet of flowers!"

Nothing happened.

All at once, Molly realised Stuart wasn't there.

He must have taken the flowers, and gone off into the garden somewhere.

Molly was going red.

She held up the wand.

Suddenly, she stared at the curtains.

They were moving.

Something was appearing through them.

Flowers. And not the plastic ones from her magic set. Real flowers, a magnificent selection of flowers, decorated with a huge satin bow.

Molly's eyes popped. She looked from the flowers, to her magic wand, to her gaping audience – and back to the flowers again.

A moment later, a pair of hands appeared through

the curtains, holding the flowers.

And a moment later, Uncle Pete stood in the doorway.

"Oh." He looked surprised. "Hello. Sorry I'm late. Problem with the car."

"Oh, brilliant!" Grandpa clapped loudly. So did the rest of the family. "And an appearing uncle, too!"

Molly laughed. She bowed.

Uncle Pete grinned.

"Sorry to barge in this way. I saw Stuart, I thought you were all in the garden." He held the flowers out to Nan. "These are for you, Mum."

"Oh, thank you!" Nan stepped forward to take them. "What a lovely surprise."

She turned to Molly.

"I think it's time for tea now," she said. "That was excellent, Molly. You're going to be a really good magician!"

Molly smiled.

"Now," Nan went on. "I've got sausage rolls and a pizza in the oven. And no one told me you already had a birthday cake. So you'll just have to eat your way through another one."

Molly grinned.

"I reckon I can manage that."

Nan looked around.

"Where *is* Stuart? Is he coming for tea too?"

"Not right now," Molly said. "Maybe later."

She smiled to herself.

"He seems to have disappeared."

The School V.I.P.

"QUIET!"

Mrs Hoskins almost screamed the word, as she stood in the doorway of her classroom.

Everyone froze.

Chaos met her eyes. Susie and Abigail were re-styling Rachel's hair in a way she obviously didn't want, and Rachel was crying. Jordon was trying to place Simon's head in the class eco-system. And five more of the boys were busy in trying to build the volumes of the *Children's Encyclopaedia* into a tower. As Mrs Hoskins yelled, the tower collapsed.

In the middle of it all, Lorinda, the classroom assistant, a tubby figure in cardigan and jeans, stood helpless, paralysed with fear.

There was a long and terrible silence.

Then Mrs Hoskins forced herself to speak calmly.

"We will deal with this in a moment. But first, I want all this mess cleared up. Everyone back at their desks. And everyone, silently reading, until I'm ready to speak to you."

She turned her glare towards Lorinda.

"Could I please have a word?"

A few minutes later, Lorinda left the large stockroom adjoining the classroom, where Mrs Hoskins kept her desk and her sanity. Lorinda's eyes were red and misty.

Mrs Hoskins stared after her through the half-open door. Couldn't she leave the class in her care for five minutes?

Mrs Hoskins grabbed her powder compact from her bag, for an emergency repair.

Her face, in the small, round mirror, looked as scarlet and angry as she felt. As soon as she stepped back into that classroom, there was going to be a storm that would make the '87 hurricane look like a summer breeze.

"Difficult, aren't they."

Mrs Hoskins jumped.

No one else was in there with her, yet a voice had spoken. In amazement, she looked from left to right.

Then she looked again into the mirror.

And what she saw made her wonder whether her class had finally tipped her over the edge.

The voice she could hear was her own.

And the face in the mirror was talking to her.

"Bit of a trial, I admit," the mirror said.

For once, Mrs Hoskins was lost for words. She was opening and shutting her mouth like a demented goldfish.

But it made no difference to the image in the mirror.

"But worth going on with," the mirror said.

It smiled.

"Oh, don't worry. And don't bother to ask questions,

that would be boring. Who are you, what are you doing in there, what's going on, you can be a bit predictable at times you know. Maybe I'm a vision, maybe I'm the voice of your conscience, it really doesn't matter.

'The point is, you need to take care of your class.

'*Because someone out there is rather more important than you might think.*"

Mrs Hoskins stared.

The mirror gave another smile.

"Look at them. Out there, where you get hurt every day. Go on. Look at them."

Mrs Hoskins pushed the stockroom door slightly. She could see many of the class now. They were all behaving themselves in the way that only came from fear. They were sitting there, pretending to read, and even Jordon was looking at a book. Albeit upside down.

The mirror grinned.

"Nice and quiet now. But what about earlier? They looked like a teacher's worst nightmare, didn't they? The sort of thing that makes you wake up sweating at five a.m., and I know you do."

Mrs Hoskins nodded dumbly.

"But someone out there," the mirror went on, "is going to do very well, in twenty or so years' time. You've got yourself a Very Important Person.

'One of them will become famous. One of them will lead this country through the most difficult time in its future history."

Mrs Hoskins stared.

"Yes," the mirror concluded. "Someone, out there

in your classroom now, is going to be Prime Minister."

Mrs Hoskins exploded into a sudden laugh. She couldn't help herself.

"Oh, no, no," the mirror said softly. "Don't laugh. It may seem crazy. But what you do now, as the teacher here, will make all the difference. Someone you see every day out there is going to be Prime Minister of the United Kingdom."

Mrs Hoskins turned to stare again through the half-open door.

"The question is…" the mirror smirked. "Who?"

Mrs Hoskins found her voice at last.

"How can I know?"

"That," the mirror said slyly. "Is for you to work out."

The image in the mirror began to fade, like a TV fading to black.

"We'll talk again."

"No!" Mrs Hoskins cried.

The image in the mirror returned. But this time, it was just an ordinary reflection. The normal red-faced Mrs Hoskins was back.

There was silence.

Slowly, dazedly, Mrs Hoskins replaced the compact in her bag.

Someone tapped softly at the door.

"Excuse me, miss." Tariq stood there, polite and respectful. He held a pile of papers in his hand. "Sorry. But someone brought these round. From the Head's office."

He handed the papers to her. From far away, Mrs Hoskins saw a pile of worksheets.

She found her voice again.

"Right… Thank you, Tariq."

Tariq peeped into the stockroom.

"Who were you talking to?"

"*Thank you, Tariq,*" Mrs Hoskins said firmly. "I'll be there in a moment."

Tariq knew what that tone of voice meant. He moved away.

Mrs Hoskins looked down at the worksheets. She blinked.

The heading read:

School Election.

"Well, I dunno," said Jordon. "I thought we were gonna get a right hammering when she came in." He jabbed a grubby thumb in the direction of the stockroom. "But she's been in there twenty minutes and she ain't come out."

"I took some work in to her," Tariq said, across the table. "She was just sitting there."

Jordon grinned.

"Tariq heard her talking to herself. Reckon she's going a bit…?" He moved his finger round his temple, and stuck out his tongue.

The other boys grinned, except for Tariq, who looked worried.

Everyone fell silent suddenly, as the stockroom door opened.

Mrs Hoskins emerged.

To everyone's surprise, she looked quite calm.

When she finally spoke, her voice was quiet.

"I will deal later with the appalling…" She checked herself. "With the… er… *unfortunate* incidents that took place this afternoon."

"Look what they've done to my hair!" Rachel wailed.

"Be quiet, Rachel," said Mrs Hoskins briskly. "What I have to talk to you about now is rather more important."

She held up the pile of worksheets.

"I have some information here from Mrs Raeburn that may interest one of you. I mean, some of you. All of you."

The class stared.

"As those of you who watch the news will know…"

The class looked blank.

"There is going to be a General Election soon. Everyone will be voting for a new Government, and a new Prime Minister. And in this school, we are going to be having a mock Election of our own. Every class has to elect its own candidate. The winners will go into the full Election in front of the whole school."

She paused, as if expecting everyone to cheer. No one did.

"So what that means," Mrs Hoskins said, "is a big opportunity."

She forced herself to smile.

"Who knows. We might even have a future Prime Minister in this class!"

There was the briefest of pauses.

Then everyone roared with laughter.

Mrs Hoskins's expression darkened. She flung the worksheets at Lorinda, who stood timidly nearby.

"Dish these out."

"Have you decided, yet?"

Mrs Hoskins jumped. She was halfway through marking books, sitting once more in the stockroom, when her own voice boomed out at her from the depths of her bag.

She fished out the compact and opened it, to see her own face smiling cheerfully back at her.

"Will you keep my voice down!" she hissed. "I mean, your voice down. The class will hear!"

"Have you worked out who it is?" the mirror asked.

Mrs Hoskins was silent. She looked through the half-open door at the class. It was almost the end of the day, and they were looking restless.

"Let's give you some help," the mirror suggested. "Who would it be? What qualities are needed in a Prime Minister?"

Mrs Hoskins paused.

"So…" she said slowly. "We're looking for someone… hard-working. Who understands people. And this country. Someone who's a good example to others. And someone who is responsible enough to lead."

The mirror was silent.

Mrs Hoskins looked across the classroom. Then she smiled.

Across the room, Tariq was quietly tidying up the stationery table, even though no one had asked him to.

"I think I've found the answer."

"Before we start this morning," Mrs Hoskins said, "I have an announcement to make."

She stood at the front of the classroom. The class was looking impatient. They were waiting to go and do P.E.

Beside Mrs Hoskins stood Tariq, looking modestly proud.

Mrs Hoskins looked down at him.

"Would you like to tell the class, Tariq?"

Tariq cleared his throat.

"Mrs Hoskins has told me -"

Mrs Hoskins cleared her throat.

"– has *asked* me," said Tariq hastily, "to put myself up as candidate for this class for the School Election."

He turned to pick up a large sheet of white paper.

"So, what do I stand for?"

He held the paper up. On it was a list he had written in red and blue marker. It was headed: TARIQ'S POLICIES.

"A vote for Tariq is a vote for a better education. I will work with the staff to make this happen. If I am elected there will be the following."

He read from the list.

"Number One. More after-school clubs. Not just in things like music and drama. There will be a Maths Club, a Science Club." He paused, impressively. "Maybe even Geography."

Jordon leaned over to his neighbour.

"You wait 'til break."

"Two," Tariq continued. "School meals. Even after the healthy eating drive, our canteen still serves far too many chips and cakes. If I am elected, I will suggest the canteen be replaced by a salad bar, with chips being served no more than four times per term."

Everyone was staring at Tariq. He seemed blissfully unaware.

"Three," said Tariq. "More special projects. Environmental and social. We need to get this school more involved in the community. I will suggest we all get involved in projects, on Saturdays and Sundays -"

Everyone was looking horror-stricken now, and one of the girls seemed about to faint.

"- in such things," Tariq went on, "as community litter-picks and the redecoration of the Children's Centre. And Four -"

Jordon picked up a large, heavy book. Just in time, he met Mrs Hoskins's eye, and Tariq was saved.

"Four," Tariq finished. "I will personally see that extra classes are available out of school hours for whoever wants them, so that we can all do well in our end-of-year tests."

There was a very, very long silence. Following the last statement, even Mrs Hoskins was struggling to look enthusiastic.

Tariq beamed at his classmates.

"Vote for me."

"This is awful!" Mrs Hoskins moaned into her compact. "How's he going to be Prime Minister? No one likes any of his ideas, no one would want to vote for them, but he's going ahead with them anyway!" She paused. "Did I just answer my own question there?"

The face in the mirror smirked.

"Are you absolutely sure that *he's* the one?"

"You mean," Mrs Hoskins gulped. "He's not?"

The mirror smiled.

"I thought I'd made it clear to you that the answer wasn't obvious. But it was the obvious answer you went for. Now, look at the class more closely. You should be looking for a less likely candidate."

Less likely?

Mrs Hoskins looked out of the stockroom door. Nearby sat Rachel. She was looking miserably down at the table, and Susie and Abigail were laughing.

"Not – ?" Mrs Hoskins looked at Rachel in disbelief. "*Her?* She never says anything! She's the quietest girl in the class! Everyone picks on her -" She stopped. "Or is that what she's going to grow away from? Is *that* what you meant by less likely?"

The mirror's smile continued.

Mrs Hoskins took a deep breath.

She put the compact down, and opened the stockroom door. Lorinda was sitting nearby, a tubby, silent presence, cutting up some coloured paper.

"Lorinda. Ask Rachel to come in, please. Now."

"I've got some exciting news," said Mrs Hoskins

unconvincingly, just before lunch. "We have another candidate."

Rachel now stood, awkwardly, by Mrs Hoskins's side. There were several stares, and the odd snigger.

"Rachel," Mrs Hoskins continued, "has decided to follow Tariq's example and put herself up for the Election."

She turned to Rachel, who was going redder by the second and looking very, very embarrassed.

"Rachel? Would you like to tell the class what policies you have?"

There was silence. Rachel stared at her shoes.

Mrs Hoskins smiled encouragingly.

"Would you like to say a few words?"

In the silence that followed, a pencil dropped and could be heard rolling across the classroom floor.

Mrs Hoskins's smile became desperate.

"Would you like to say… anything? Please?"

She turned to the class.

"Anyone want to say anything? About… anything? At all?"

Silence.

Finally, Mrs Hoskins said:

"Right. Lunch, then."

Within ten seconds, the classroom was empty.

"She can't be the one!" Mrs Hoskins cried. She could afford some volume now. The class was still at lunch.

From the mirror, her own face grinned back at her.

"So, if she's not the one…" Mrs Hoskins found a handkerchief, and mopped her brow. "Who? There's no one else, that I can think of…"

She stared into the mirror. That smirk was still there, and she had the sudden urge to slap her own face.

"Remember what I said," the mirror said. "A less likely candidate."

The mirror paused.

"You might even say – the *least* likely."

There was silence.

Then Mrs Hoskins's eyes bulged.

"Oh – what? Oh no! No, no! No way!"

Mrs Hoskins gritted her teeth as she stood before the class.

"Meet Jordon."

She held onto a nearby chair for support.

"Your new candidate."

Beside her stood the large and ungainly presence that was Jordon. He was loving the attention, and grinning.

"Jordon. Would you like to explain your policies?"

Jordon swaggered forward.

"Right. I want you all to vote for me. And anyone who don't, will get their head knocked off. OK?"

The smaller class members nodded meekly.

"Here's my policies." Jordon held up a large, torn piece of corrugated cardboard. On it was a picture of an umbrella and This Way Up. He hastily turned it over.

His policies were scrawled on the other side, in black felt tip.

"One. An opt-out of Maths and English, and extra P.E. for those what don't want to do 'em. Two. From now on, all Detentions to take place in a special room. That room to contain a widescreen TV, DVD player and a games console. And Four -"

Simon sniggered, then stopped as Jordon looked at him.

"*Four*," said Jordon firmly. "Classes can vote on whether their teachers are any good or not. And if they're not… we can get rid of 'em." He turned to Mrs Hoskins. "Two-thirds majority and you're out, miss."

He turned back to the class.

"So vote for me!"

There was a pause.

Then two-thirds of the class cheered.

Mrs Hoskins shut her eyes.

She also kept them shut for a lot of the time on the day of the School Election.

She sat on the stage, with the other class teachers. The whole school was assembled in the Hall. There were some parents – parents! – there too, who were looking bemused. Lorinda stood dismally by, guarding a table of tea, biscuits and orange squash.

Seven rows back from the stage sat the class. Tariq was looking annoyed. Rachel was looking relieved.

And on the stage stood Jordon, wearing a large badge that said "CLASS CANDIDATE".

"The future of education," said Jordon, who seemed to be warming to his role, "belongs to youth. And what I want is for all of yous lot to come with me. As we start to break the teachers' power. A vote for me is a vote what makes school fun."

He grinned at the school.

"Are you gonna vote for me, then?"

The response nearly blew the roof off.

"YES!"

There were cheers and applause – from the kids. The parents were looking uncomfortable. The other teachers looked thunderstruck.

On stage, Mrs Raeburn leaned over to Mrs Hoskins.

"Could you spare time for a little chat in my office afterwards? Thank you *so* much."

"He won!" Mrs Hoskins staggered into her classroom.

She looked redder than ever. The little chat had not been a pleasant one.

She found herself addressing the only other person in there – Lorinda.

The kids were still in the Hall, eating, drinking and congratulating Jordon on his victory.

"Jordon won the School Election!"

"Well, that's good." Lorinda paused. "Isn't it?"

She caught Mrs Hoskins's eye.

"I mean… you wanted him to win. Didn't you? That's what all the class were saying…"

"What do you know about it?" Mrs Hoskins

rounded on her. "What do you know about anything? Think you'd ever make a teacher? You can't even cut paper straight, let alone control a class. And, sweetheart, if by some miracle you do ever manage to get any further in the education system, I personally will campaign to put kids back up chimneys!"

With that, she stormed into the stockroom and slammed the door.

"Why did I ever do it?" Mrs Hoskins raged at her reflection. "Why did I ever let you influence me? The worst boy in the class, the worst boy in the school, probably, wins the School Election. And because *I* put him up as a candidate! I'll never be able to face those parents again…"

She stopped. All at once, the face in the mirror was fading.

And another face was taking its place.

It was the face of another woman, young, calm, good-looking. Even beautiful.

It was her own face, again. But from years before. When she had just started teaching.

When the job had seemed so good…

"Mrs Hoskins?"

The new woman spoke.

"I am sorry, Mrs Hoskins. I'm afraid you've been misled. The premonition you were supposed to receive was not given to you in the proper manner, leading to your acting wrongly as a result. You've been the victim of what we in the spirit world call a Macbeth Situation.

But don't worry. Disciplinary action is being taken."

Mrs Hoskins staggered.

"What you were first told is true," the new woman admitted. "Someone you see in your class *will* be Prime Minister."

A pause.

"But not one of the pupils."

The new face faded, and in the mirror, Mrs Hoskins saw another image.

It was an image she recognised, from endless news programmes. It was 10 Downing Street.

Assembled crowds were cheering. And, outside the famous black door, a rather tubby woman in a grey suit was smiling and waving.

It was obviously many years into the future. But it was Lorinda.

"It may interest you to know," said the new woman's voice, "that Lorinda does have a life outside your classroom. As a matter of fact, she's very active in local politics. Oh, it's making the coffee now. Putting leaflets into envelopes. But in five years' time, she'll be a local Councillor. Ten years and she'll be a Member of Parliament."

The image faded, and the new face returned.

"And when she finally retires from politics, she'll write her book. It'll be a bestseller. And you, Mrs Hoskins, won't even get a mention. Except maybe in one short paragraph, where she talks about the nastiness and the bullying she suffered in her early career in education."

The face hardened.

"I'm sorry. You've missed your chance."

Mrs Hoskins flung open the door into the classroom.

But the classroom was empty.

Lorinda had gone.

Lorinda served twelve years as Prime Minister.

Jordon served twelve days as Pupil Representative, before resigning over an expenses claim for mobile phone calls and chocolate bars.

Rachel learned to play the cello, and later would play in orchestras all over the world.

And Tariq gave up politics and went on to become a doctor.

Everyone still said how good he was.

Spot the Difference

George entered the room, looking sulky. He went straight across and took his place at his desk, next to Tim.

"How did it go?" Tim inquired.

"It's not fair." George looked down at the desk. "They're blaming me for the whole thing. They said I didn't plan it properly, and I've let everybody down."

"It wasn't your fault," Tim put in mildly.

George's mood didn't lift.

"Now I've got to go and see Beamish, at twelve o'clock. While *she*…" (his brow furrowed), "gets away with it as usual."

He fell silent as Octavia passed by. She had a new hairstyle and was looking pleased with herself.

She gave George the most sarcastic of smiles before returning to her own desk.

"It's not right," George went on, in a low voice. "I thought of this Project. I planned the whole thing. Did all the work. And then *she* had to butt in." He scowled. "Changed the whole thing. Never a *word* to me. And then it all goes wrong, and *I* end up taking the blame."

He fell silent as he realised Octavia was watching him.

His face was thunderous as he returned to his work.

Eleven fifty-nine saw George waiting outside the heavy door marked: "Mr. BEAMISH". His mouth was dry and he could feel his heart pounding.

He straightened his tie.

He glanced at his watch, just at the moment when eleven fifty-nine changed to twelve.

"IN!" bellowed a voice beyond the door. George jumped.

He hadn't even knocked…

Very slowly, he reached for the door handle.

It was an unhappy, rather than an angry George who returned to Tim that afternoon.

Tim was busy with computer work. There was an awkward silence as he saw George.

Finally, Tim broke it.

"Are you coming out tonight, then?"

"No," muttered George. "I've got to stay late." His eyes narrowed in the direction of Octavia. She had obviously seen George's expression, and was talking to some of the girls – and laughing.

"Come out at the weekend, then," Tim suggested. "We could go bowling – haven't done that for ages. We could have a burger, afterwards."

George said nothing. As he headed back to his desk, he aimed a kick at the waste-paper bin.

"I *hate* this place."

George stayed late. Did some extra work.

He stared dismally out of the window. It was starting to get dark.

Tim would be with his family at the cinema by now. Octavia would be out somewhere with her girly friends, telling them for the umpteenth time how clever she'd been.

Everyone else had gone home long ago.

Finally, it was over.

The caretaker was still in the building as George headed for the exit. He gave George a sympathetic look.

"Good night, George."

"Good night."

The caretaker turned to lock up.

George breathed a sigh of relief. It was over, for another day.

Briskly, George walked out of the office block, got into his car and drove away.

"How was your day?" his wife, Jackie asked a short time later. Like George, she had had to work late. She sat in the front passenger seat of the car, and leaned over to give her husband a quick kiss on the cheek before they drove away.

George made no reply.

"Octavia again?" Jackie smiled gently. "I don't know why you put up with her."

"You shouldn't let her get to you, Dad," his eleven-year-old son, Marc said from the back seat. George had collected him from swimming club and he had his bag on the seat beside him. The car stank of chlorine. "She's only doing it to get attention. If you let her see she's getting to you, she'll only get worse. Best thing to do is just ignore her."

Marc turned to look out of the side window. The traffic was heavy, and a car near to them was hooting. Someone somewhere was shouting at a fellow motorist.

It was a cold, dank night and condensation was beginning to form on the window. Marc started to draw pictures in it idly with his finger.

"After all," he muttered to himself. "She's just a grown-up…"

Snowed In

Out of the night sky came the swirling blizzard. Massive white flakes spiralled across the town, covering roads, gardens, pathways.

In the back room of a terraced house, Liam stood at the window, watching as the world outside disappeared beneath the blanket of snow.

"No sign of it stopping," he said.

He turned back to face the room. But the room was hardly visible. There was no light, no electric fire, no television.

Amidst the darkness he could just make out a stocky figure lying sprawled on the leather sofa. The figure made no reply.

Liam sniffed.

"My Dad says we're the only country in the world what's never ready for snow. Few flakes come down. And everything stops."

There was still no reply from the sofa. Liam hadn't heard anything from the figure lying there for several minutes. He could just make out the outline, the back of a head of dark hair.

"Including the power," Liam went on. "There was so much on TV tonight. And we were gonna play on the games console." He aimed a kick at the skirting board beneath the window. "Haven't even been able to have any proper tea."

"It'll come back on, soon." The boy on the sofa spoke at last. He raised his mobile phone to eye level, the screen providing a tiny spot of intense light in the darkened room. He was texting. Liam could see the hand holding the phone, the cuff of the tracksuit jacket beneath. "Just gotta be patient."

The door opened and, invisibly, Justin walked in.

"There's nothing happening out front," his voice said to Liam. "No cars. Nobody about. Everyone's indoors, like us."

Liam had fetched out his own phone and was scanning the room with it. It lit up the pictures on the wall... the mess of boxed games and toys cluttering the carpet... the newspapers and magazines covering the table. It lit up Justin, as he crossed the room. And it lit up Lewis, lying on the sofa.

Liam took a look at the brothers. Even though Lewis was sixteen, a lot older than Justin, it was weird just how alike they were. Lewis looked like a projection of Justin's future self.

Liam made a mental note to keep Justin playing football. Otherwise, in a few years' time he'd be living on the sofa as well.

"They're having their tea, opposite." Justin sat on a handy beanbag.

"Lucky old them." Liam scanned a tray on the floor, which was covered with the remains of their makeshift supper. There were a few tins and packets. Anything they'd managed to loot from the store cupboard. "I thought that's what *I* was coming here for. Some night out this is."

"I was only doing beans on toast for you all, anyway." Lewis reached down a hand to the tray and lifted a giant can of beans. "You're welcome to 'em cold, if you want."

It was lucky he couldn't see Liam's face.

They heard the phone replaced in the hall.

Another, shorter figure appeared in the doorway.

"That was Mum," a small girl's voice said. "She said, the play got cancelled, they're all stuck in traffic and it's not moving. They'll be home as soon as they can."

Liam glanced again at the food store. "What did I have, for my tea? Four cream crackers. A can of cold frankfurters. And half a bar of chocolate marzipan."

"I liked it," the girl's voice said. "It was much nicer than a *normal* meal."

Liam flinched as suddenly, her face lit up. She was holding a battery-operated camping lantern.

"I found it," Abbie told her brothers. She set the lantern down in a central position. "It was under the stairs."

"Oh, nice one," Lewis approved.

Liam could see the three of them now. In the dim, amber light their faces looked quite eerie.

He sat on a stool by the TV. The television screen had been left blank and cold and empty, just like every other electrical device.

"Weird, innit?" Justin broke into Liam's thoughts. "How much we need stuff. Stuff that uses electricity. You don't realise 'til the power goes off. All the things we need, just to live. Fridge. Cooker. Games system."

"Does anyone want some more food?" Abbie bustled around with the air of someone hosting a party.

"I'll have the sausage roll, if no one wants it," Lewis told her.

"I've not had my pudding, yet." Justin reached for the food tray and picked up what was left of a large jar of blackberry jam. He took a spoon and lolled back on the beanbag, eating the jam straight from the jar. Lewis bit into the flattened and unheated sausage roll.

Liam turned his head so as not to show his disgust.

There was silence.

"Reckon school's gonna be closed on Monday?" Justin asked, with his mouth full.

"Nah." Liam stood up again, and returned to the window. "We couldn't get that lucky. I bet you it all thaws tomorrow night, just in time for us to go in on Monday morning."

He peered across the thickening blanket of snow covering the back yard of Justin's house.

"That's if we're not still stuck here."

"They'll have to pay me overtime for the extra work, if you are," Lewis said, without moving. "They're only paying me a tenner for babysitting you lot. And it runs out at ten-thirty."

Liam snorted.

"What! We're babysitting *you*, you mean."

"No, *I'm* babysitting *you*."

"No way!"

"No," Abbie said firmly. "*I* think I'm definitely babysitting all of *you*."

Even though she was the smallest, none of them quite dared to argue.

"What shall we do, then?" Justin asked. "'Til they get back?"

"Dunno." Liam held the TV guide close to the lantern. The batteries were failing. "You won't believe how much stuff we've missed."

"What about I-Spy?" Justin suggested.

Liam laughed sarcastically.

"Oh yeah, sure. I spy with my little eye, something beginning with D. Darkness. Hooray! Your turn."

There was a long silence.

"Hey." Abbie brightened. "I know. Make our own entertainment."

"You what?" Liam asked.

Abbie grinned.

"Do a show." She turned to her brothers. "Like we do for Nana."

"What?" Liam asked.

Justin smiled.

"Sometimes, right, on birthdays and things, when the family's round. We do a show. Always have done. Everyone has to get up and do something."

"I'm up for it." Lewis surfaced. "Anything to keep you little kids happy."

"We've got no proper light, though," Justin frowned.
Abbie smiled.

"Yes we have."

"She's clever, ain't she?" Lewis asked Liam a couple
of minutes later. He shifted a couple of books on the
high shelf. Into the space, he carefully wedged the
large, powerful torch Abbie had borrowed from their
Dad's toolbox.

He switched it on, sending a dazzling shaft of light
down into the centre of the room, where they'd cleared
a space.

It did look uncannily like a spotlight.

"Yeah," Liam agreed. He grinned. "I dunno where
she gets it from."

"Are you ready?" called an imperious voice from
the hallway. "Remember – I'm on first!"

"'Course!" Lewis shouted. He rolled his eyes.

"Audience in place?" Abbie shouted.

Liam and Justin hastily made for their seats, while
Lewis took centre stage.

"Ladies and gentlemen! Good evening and welcome
to the show. This is one performance they're not gonna
cancel tonight!"

He was holding the spoon from Justin's jam jar, as
an imaginary microphone.

"And the pressure's on, as we introduce our first
act. Ladies and gentlemen – all the way from the hall –
it's ABBIE!"

Liam and Justin cheered as the door opened and

Abbie twirled her way in. She had put on her ballet skirt.

Lewis joined the other boys in the audience, as Abbie went into her song and dance routine.

Liam found himself oddly impressed. She had no music, and must have been making up the dance moves as she went along. She was singing, too. He wasn't sure what. It could have been something in the charts. It could have been a nursery rhyme. But whatever it was, it sounded good.

Abbie did a final pirouette and went into a big finish, small arms flung out to either side.

The boys applauded, while a beaming Abbie flushed and curtseyed.

"Thank you, Abbie!" Lewis went over to his little sister as she came off, giving her a quick hug. "You're a star."

He returned to the stage.

"And now, the tallest boy in Juniper Class, all the way from somewhere near the roof – it's LIAM!"

Justin cheered and, taking her seat in the audience, so did Abbie.

"You what?" Liam rose, embarrassed.

"We told you the rules," Lewis reminded. "*Everyone* has to do something."

"I don't *do* nothing," Liam protested.

He paused.

"Hey. Hang on. Hang on."

He went to the scattered toys and games. From Abbie's tiny toy snooker table, he picked up three balls, a red, the green and the pink.

Walking back to the stage area, he started to juggle them.

"Oh, nice one." As usual, Justin was there in support. "Go Liam! Go Liam!"

Liam threw the green ball in the air, then, with a deft movement, caught it with the bridge of his nose. He rolled it backwards and forwards, all the while juggling the other two balls.

"Excellent!" Lewis the compère moved over to Liam. "Well done, Liam! *Come* on!"

He gave Liam a friendly slap on the back. Liam jumped.

The red ball flew across the room and there was the sound of something breaking.

After a brief pause, all four of them decided not to say anything.

Liam returned to his seat.

"Who's next, then?"

"Come on, Justin!" Abbie said. "Do your impressions."

"What?" Liam sounded surprised.

"Oh, you'll like these," Lewis said. "He does 'em in every show."

Liam looked at his best mate in surprise.

"I never knew you done impressions, J."

With a secret smile, Justin took the stage. Lewis and Abbie applauded.

"Ladies and gentlemen. As I was walking along the street on my way here tonight -"

"You *live* here," Liam protested.

"- Shut up -" Justin told him, "- I met several well-known personalities. And who's the first person we see coming along here?"

He paused momentarily, and spoke in a deep, posh voice.

"Good evening. The headlines tonight!"

Lewis and Abbie grinned. Liam looked bewildered.

"Who was it?"

Justin frowned.

"He reads the news. On satellite."

"*I've* never heard of him!" Liam objected. "Do another one."

Justin shrugged.

"OK. Then, moving on down the street, who should I see but this fine gentleman."

He had a very, very bad go at a Scouse accent.

"A'right, kidder? Your Mum sent you shopping, 'as she? Need some chops."

Liam looked at Justin as if he'd just beamed down from Mars.

"Who was that?"

He turned to see Lewis looking at him in amazement.

"It's old Chambers, of course!"

"*Who?*" Liam cried.

"The butcher!" Justin insisted. "Down Bridge Street. Place where we get our chump chops and sausages."

"Oh." Lewis rubbed his belly longingly. "Don't."

"How am *I* meant to know?" Liam demanded.

Justin looked indignant.

"Well, it sounds just like him. You don't seem to know how impressions work."

This time, he went on with the act without being asked.

"And then, outside his house, who should I see but -"

He spoke in his own voice, but deeper.

"Are you three gonna tidy up that room, or what? If I find stuff everywhere again, you're all gonna be grounded, *no* problem!"

Liam stared.

"Go on then. Who was it?"

Abbie looked very hurt.

"Our Dad!"

"Well, *he's* not famous!" Liam yelled. "Who knows *him*?"

"*Everyone* knows our Dad," Abbie said severely. "He takes them their mail."

"All the way up Chalford Road!" Justin added. "In all weathers. *And* round by the park." He sounded really put out now. "No one else can do an impression of him. I'm the only one in the whole world."

This time, Liam found himself incapable of speech. He had his eyes shut, as if in pain.

Quietly, Justin returned to his seat.

"Mum's always loved that one."

"Right then!" Lewis headed back to the stage. "My turn."

From his pocket, he took a plastic kazoo and blew an ear-splitting blast.

"What do you want, then? The National Anthem or some modern jazz?"

"Right!" Liam leapt to his feet. "Show's over! Thanks for having me!"

He made a dash for the door.

"Where are you going?" Justin demanded.

"Home!" Liam shouted. "Even if I have to ski!"

Lewis turned away in disgust, while Abbie looked ready to cry. Even Justin looked narked.

"You're a right misery, you are, Liam. We have you over, put a show on for you… "

He stopped. Liam was standing still.

"Having their tea?" he said.

"What?" Justin frowned.

"The house opposite!" Liam went on. "You said they was having their tea… how d'you know? How could you see into their house?"

"Well, the light was on," Justin said.

His hand flew to his mouth.

Liam flung the door open, and both of them ran from the room.

"You *twit*!"

Lewis and Abbie stayed put. They heard Liam's voice echoing back.

"They've got their lights on! *Everyone's* got their lights on! Why aren't ours working?"

The voices interrupted by the sound of an opening front door.

"We're back!" It was the voice of Lewis, Justin and Abbie's Mum. "Sorry we were so long. At least it's stopped snowing now." A pause. "Why are you all in the dark?"

Lewis and Abbie headed for the hall.

"There was a power cut," Lewis said.

"Oh, we've just seen Sandra," their Mum said. "Power came back on ages ago."

Their Dad flicked a light switch.

"Must have been a fuse," he said, in his deep voice. "Fuse went, didn't it? That's why our lights never came back on."

He headed for the fuse box.

"Soon fix that, *no* problem."

"See," Justin said to Liam.

"Then we -" Liam seemed to be fighting some deep emotional battle. "All the time – we was eating cold food -"

A few moments later, the lights came on. Liam blinked at the family he could suddenly see standing all around him.

"Well, we're in now." Mum took her coat off. "Who cares about the weather?" She headed for the kitchen. "You poor things, haven't you had any proper tea? I'll make you something now."

"Yay!" Abbie did a little leap and the boys looked pleased.

"I think there's some pizza in the freezer," Mum went on. "Pepperoni… better use it up."

"Excellent!" Liam followed, beaming.

"Oh…" Mum frowned. "Sorry, Liam… your Mum and Dad are waiting for you in the car. You've got to go now."

"LIAM!" Liam's Dad's voice yelled from outside. "Come on! This car's freezing up!"

Liam's face said it all.

Lewis and Abbie were struggling not to laugh.

"Never mind, Liam," Justin said. "Another time, yeah?"

He clenched his fist and gave Liam a friendly nudge.

"Tell you what, mate. Next Saturday… We could all come round to your house instead."

The New Pupil

"That's lovely, Miranda." Miss Havers stood back and looked at the finished display with a grateful smile. "Thank you *so* much."

Miranda smiled proudly.

In the centre of the wall, large, green letters, painstakingly cut out by Miranda, proclaimed: "HOW WE'RE BEING GREEN". Around the lettering, images of wind turbines and reusable carrier bags gave their message to the school.

Most of the drawings had been done by Miranda, and all of them had been trimmed and pasted onto coloured paper by her.

It was easily the best display in the whole of the Hall.

"I don't know where this class would be without you, sometimes." Miss Havers breathed a sigh of relief. "Do you know, your classmates have had *three whole weeks* to come up with something? I give them time to work on a display. And what do I find? Two half-completed essays and a drawing of a penguin. Still." She smiled brightly at Miranda. "I knew *you'd* be able to pull it together. Five team points, I think."

Miranda went out alone into the yard.

But she wasn't alone for long.

"Miranda!" Carrie came dashing up. "Can you help me with my Maths homework? It's Maths next, but I don't know what on earth I'm doing with binary."

"Miranda!" Rosie and Nancy, two of the smaller girls called to her from the playing field. "Come and help us untangle our skipping rope?"

"Miranda!" a small boy shouted. "I've lost 70p!"

"Wait 'til we go back in, Sam." Miranda smiled at him. "I'll be coming round all the classrooms. That's the time to report lost money."

Sam looked happier at once.

Miranda sighed. All these people, coming at her with their problems.

It wasn't that she minded. In fact, she enjoyed helping people.

The trouble was, everyone knew that. Pupils and teachers. Whenever help was needed at a parents' evening, or with the scenery for a school play, everyone shouted for Miranda. And Miranda found it very difficult to say no.

It wasn't as if she didn't have worries of her own to sort out.

For the umpteenth time that day, she took the form from her pocket. The Sponsored Walk. She and the Youth Group from the church were supposed to be doing it that Saturday. And so far, Miranda's sponsor form contained fifty pence promised from Patsy, 20p each from the twins, and Danny had just written: "No chance".

It was rather a different story when Miranda wanted people to do something for *her*...

"Not fair, is it?"

Miranda jumped. The voice was coming from behind her.

She turned.

Standing there was a tall girl of about her own age, with long dark hair and a very big smile. Miranda had seen her once or twice lately, lurking in the corner of the playground. Never with anyone, never talking, never joining in any of the games. Just watching.

She couldn't have been at the school for long, or Miranda would have seen her before now. Miranda wondered which class she was in.

She was grateful for sympathy, anyway. She smiled back at the girl.

"How much have you collected?" The girl reached out and plucked the sponsor form from Miranda's hand. She grinned. "Less than a pound? Out of all the people here? And all the nice things you do for them. Not fair, is it?"

"No," Miranda admitted. "Sorry, I don't know your name?"

The girl made no reply. She returned the form.

Miranda paused.

"Would *you* like to sponsor me?"

"I *could*." The girl smiled again. "Anything's possible."

Miranda shuddered, very slightly.

There was something odd about the girl's smile. Something creepy...

"Of course," the girl went on. "There'd have to be… conditions."

Miranda hesitated again.

She tried to sound businesslike.

"How much would you be willing to sponsor me for?"

"In return for meeting the conditions?" the girl went on. "Oh…"

She took something from her coat pocket, and Miranda's eyes widened.

The girl was holding a bundle of ten pound notes.

"Say fifty quid?" She crinkled the money in front of Miranda. "That would solve your problem, wouldn't it? *And* do a lot of good for the children at the hospital."

"So…" Miranda blinked. "What would you want me to do in return?"

"Enough for now." The girl returned the money to her pocket. The bell had gone, and everyone was starting to line up. "But I'll be at the school gate. At hometime. If you're still interested then… meet me there."

Miranda stood a few moments longer, so stunned she was unable to move.

By the time she came round, and moved into line with the other kids, the girl was nowhere to be seen.

For once, Miranda found it hard to concentrate in Maths and Technology.

Who was that girl? Whose class was she in? And how come she had so much money – and in school?

Miranda felt uncomfortable. She didn't trust the girl.

But that money would make Miranda the greatest sponsored walker of them all...

When the bell rang, Miranda went off alone, talking to no one.

She headed straight for the gate.

And sure enough, the girl was there.

"You came!" The girl smiled. She paused. "Well?"

"OK." Miranda spoke quickly. "What do you want me to do?"

The girl said nothing. Instead, she took Miranda's arm, and led her out of the gate. She was unexpectedly strong, and Miranda found herself moving whether she wanted to or not.

"I've been watching you," the girl continued.

"I've noticed," Miranda muttered.

"Ever since I came here," the girl went on. "It's always *you*, isn't it? Being nice to people. Always doing the right thing. And never getting anything in return."

"Guess," Miranda said. It was uncanny. This girl seemed to know just what she was thinking...

"But..." the girl went on. "Have you ever thought what it would be like... just for once... not to obey the rules? Not to do what everyone tells you. Have you ever thought... of breaking a few rules?"

She looked straight into Miranda's eyes.

"Just for fun?"

Miranda looked at her, uneasily.

"How d'you mean?"

"Oh…" The girl smiled again. "There's all sorts of possibilities. We could start with something small. But to get your fifty quid… You'd really have to earn it."

She released her hold on Miranda's arm. It was no longer necessary. Miranda was now walking quite willingly with her.

"It would be good for you," the girl went on. "It would show everyone that you're you. Not just someone made up of rules, and duties. Give yourself a bit of freedom."

Miranda found herself smiling back. That certainly sounded good.

"So… what do you want me to do first?"

The girl stopped walking, and faced Miranda. She looked Miranda up and down.

"Very neat, aren't you?" She fixed her eyes on Miranda's immaculate school uniform. Carelessly, she put out a hand, pulled Miranda's tie askew, and flicked one of her plaits to the side. "Always in uniform. Always perfect…"

She hesitated, momentarily.

"I think we'll make the uniform the first step."

Miranda blinked.

"What do you mean?"

The girl smirked.

"Come in your own clothes tomorrow."

"Something as different from your uniform as possible," the girl instructed.

They had reached the gate of Miranda's house.

"Wear something that's *you*. If you're going to break a rule. *Really* break it."

Miranda was looking at the ground.

"And," the girl finished. "Remember what's at stake."

With that, she was gone.

Slowly, Miranda opened the gate and headed for the house.

It was morning. Miranda looked in the bedroom mirror.

She was wearing a bright pink top, pale pink leggings and silver sandals.

And, dressed like that, she was going to school.

It was the first time in her whole school career she had not been perfectly uniformed at this time of the morning.

People had even made fun of her, at school, for being so well turned out. The boys would make the knots in their ties too large, or too small, or have their shirts hanging out, while the girls would try to get away with makeup, or jewellery. Not Miranda.

But the class would never see Miranda, that perfectly-dressed, blameless girl, again.

Miranda took a deep breath. There wasn't time to change now.

She had to go through with it.

Everyone else had left the house by the time she finally plucked up the courage to go. That was good, in a way. Mum would never have let her go out looking like that.

But what would the teachers say?

Only the thought of presenting fifty pounds sponsor money kept her moving.

At the corner of the street, she found the girl waiting for her.

Her face broke into a smirk as soon as she saw Miranda.

"Wow!" Her smirk became a grin. "You have done well. Somehow, I never thought you'd be... so *bold*."

She took Miranda's arm in her vice-like grip.

"Come on."

The bell had gone by the time they arrived at school, and the yard was empty.

"I'm late," Miranda muttered.

"Relax," the girl told her. "Remember... there are no rules now. This is the new Miranda. You're going to be you, for a change."

She released Miranda's arm.

"You're on your own now. You've got to do this for yourself."

She took a step away.

"See you at break."

As usual, she seemed just to disappear, like a breeze, like an echo.

Miranda took a deep breath.

Then she walked into the school.

She looked neither left nor right, nor at the few people she passed, but marched straight into her classroom.

She waited for the gasps, the sniggers, then the laughter and cries.

But none came.

"Oh, Miranda!" Miss Havers rushed forward, a relieved smile on her face. She seemed not even to notice how late Miranda was. "Thank goodness *someone* realised. I knew I could rely on you."

For the first time, Miranda looked at the class.

Half of them were wearing their own clothes. Tracksuits and trainers, and tops and jeans.

The other half were in uniform as usual, and were looking annoyed.

"I totally forgot," Miss Havers confided quietly to Miranda. She picked up a sheaf of typed letters from her desk. "Totally forgot to give these out. We're the only class in the school who didn't know today was Non Uniform Day. Of course, some heard from other classes, brothers and sisters and so on… I hope you've remembered your pound."

She smiled.

"I knew I could rely on *you* to set an example."

"That wasn't supposed to happen!" The girl was waiting for Miranda at break. She grabbed Miranda's arm, and led her away towards the netball court.

"Well…" Miranda was grinning. She couldn't help herself. The relief was all over her face. "It did. And now no one knows I was meant to be being bad."

"*Listen to me!*" The girl grabbed Miranda by the shoulders.

Miranda gasped as the girl slammed her bodily into the wall. Her strength was unbelievable.

The girl put her face right up to Miranda's.

"If you want something from me, *you'll do exactly as you're told.*"

She released Miranda equally suddenly, and turned away.

"I won't be beaten."

"Beaten?" Miranda rubbed her shoulder painfully. "Who by?"

The girl said nothing.

Very quickly, her smile was returning.

"I know what we'll do next."

All at once, her voice was gentle again.

"Come with me."

Miranda found herself standing in one of the school corridors.

Once again, she felt uncomfortable. She knew she wasn't meant to be in the school building at break.

"Why are we here?"

The girl led her past the Infants' fish tank, past their mini-library and to the corridor that led to main reception.

She pointed to a red rectangular panel on the wall.

"*That's* why."

Miranda looked horrified.

"The fire alarm?"

"Just break the glass." The girl smiled. "Your next step to the new you. Your next step to fifty pounds."

"But I can't..." Miranda looked at the girl wildly. "Everyone's outside, anyway."

"The Juniors are," the girl pointed out. "Different times, for morning break. The Infants are still in their classrooms." She smiled nastily. "The ones who'll be most scared."

She produced the five ten-pound notes from her pocket.

She looked straight at Miranda, her eyes glittering.

"Just break the glass..."

She picked up the little metal hammer that hung on a chain by the alarm point. She handed it to Miranda.

"Fifty pounds..."

Under the girl's gaze, Miranda wilted.

Slowly, as if in a dream, she raised the hammer.

The glass was broken before she even knew what she'd done.

The next moment, her eardrums seemed to split. One of the klaxons was right above Miranda's head.

Miranda found herself drowning in a tidal wave of Infants, as their teachers and assistants led them out.

No! Miranda wanted to cry. *It's not a real emergency! It was me! I did it!*

She stayed silent.

She turned to look at the girl.

But the girl had gone.

"Miranda!" Mrs Raeburn, the Head had appeared. "Thank goodness! About time someone raised the alarm! Honestly, I don't know what planet some people..." She checked herself quickly. "Thank goodness half the school is out there already."

Miranda sniffed suddenly.

She could smell smoke…

"What's happening, miss?"

"Problem in the kitchen." Mrs Raeburn led Miranda away. "It's that toaster playing up again."

She smiled at Miranda as they headed for the yard.

"Thank goodness *someone* had some presence of mind."

Miranda didn't see the girl again that day.

By the time hometime arrived, she had had enough. She ran home, and up to her bedroom.

With a deep sigh of relief, she flung herself onto the bed.

"Had enough already?"

Miranda screamed.

The girl was sitting in the chair by her bed!

"But…" Miranda gulped. "How did you – ?"

"Oh, save it," the girl ordered. "I'll always be here. As long as our agreement stands. Fifty pounds. But first, you have to do something bad. You won't go on being saved forever."

"I've changed my mind!" Miranda rounded on the girl. "I won't do it!"

"*Oh yes you will.*" The girl grabbed Miranda's plaits and pulled them hard. Tears sprang to Miranda's eyes. "*Or shall I go to Mrs Raeburn and tell her why you really rang the fire alarm? For money? For a dare?*"

Miranda blinked away the tears.

Her voice, when it came, was no more than a whisper.

"Let me go…"

"Not a chance." The girl leaned back smugly in the chair. "You're going to do exactly as I tell you. And the final test comes… tomorrow morning."

Miranda was too weary even to ask what that final test might be.

She sank back onto the bed, and closed her eyes.

By the time she opened them again, the girl had gone.

Next morning, Miranda left the house early. She wanted to avoid the girl.

She was wearing uniform again, and looked exactly like her old self. And with all her heart, she wanted to be that old Miranda again.

She didn't even care about the fifty pounds any more…

But, as she turned into Station Road, the road that led to the school, her heart sank.

The girl was barring her way.

"Right," the girl commanded. She seized Miranda by the arm. "Final test starts here. The school's going to see how it can get on without Miss Perfect for the day."

"What now?" Miranda whined. "What do you mean?"

"What I mean is," the girl smirked. "You're not going to school. You're skiving off."

"No!" Miranda howled. "I've never… I've hardly ever been off sick, even!"

"First time for everything." The girl marched Miranda into a side street. "First step is to get as far away from the school as possible. We'll go to the shops. Or the park. Anywhere. It doesn't matter. *As long as you do something bad.*"

They turned into another side street, and then another. Soon, they were a good half-mile from the school.

Miranda's watch beeped. It was only fifteen minutes now until school started.

"And you can turn that off for a start," the girl ordered.

Miranda felt the tears spring to her eyes again.

She blinked around her. She didn't know this area all that well.

Nearby, a front door was opening. A Mum was leaving the house, ready to take her daughter to school, and Miranda saw that it was little Rosie. And with them was a tiny boy, a toddler. Rosie's brother, she supposed.

She stared.

The little boy was wandering away from Rosie and her Mum. Neither of them had noticed. Rosie had got something round her mouth, jam or something from breakfast, and her Mum was fussing over her, wiping it off.

Neither of them was watching the toddler.

The next moment, he was on the pavement.

The next moment, he was in the road.

Miranda started forward in panic. But the girl had seen what was happening too. She held Miranda's arm tightly.

"Leave him," she commanded. "He's nothing to do with you."

"But…" Miranda made a desperate effort to get free.

"*I said leave him.*"

Miranda stared wildly.

A car had rounded the bend of the road. It was moving fast, and trees and parked cars were blocking its view.

And the toddler was now right in the middle of the road.

The car was heading straight for him!

"*No!*"

With a final pull, Miranda was free.

As she ran forward, the girl made a grab for her.

"NO! Miranda! Don't do it! I'm warning you! This is your last chance…!"

"Go away!" Miranda screamed.

She pushed the girl aside.

"*Just go away!*"

And then she was darting forward, and seizing the little boy by the arm, and pulling him aside…

Miranda was still shouting: "*Go away!*" as she landed hard in the road.

The car sped harmlessly by…

"I'm very proud of you, Miranda," Mrs Raeburn said.

Miranda stood shakily before the Head's desk. Her ankle hurt, and she had a nasty graze to her right elbow.

"Rosie's mother told me the full story," Mrs Raeburn went on. "What you did was not only public-spirited, but extremely brave. If a little foolhardy. You could have been badly hurt."

"I had to do it," Miranda whispered. She cleared her throat quickly. "I mean…I…yeah."

"If you're willing," Mrs Raeburn said. "I'd like to call a special Assembly. Tell everyone what you've done."

Miranda hesitated.

"If you don't mind, miss… I'd rather we didn't."

"Modest as well." Mrs Raeburn shook her head in admiration. "If only I had more like you. Well. The very least I can do is… oh… say ten team points. And…"

She took out her purse.

"I believe you're collecting for a Sponsored Walk."

Miranda's face brightened.

"Shall we say… five pounds?"

Miranda's face fell.

About to leave the Head's office, Miranda paused.

"Mrs Raeburn…" she started.

"Yes?" The Head smiled back from her desk.

"Who's that girl?" Miranda asked. "The new one? My age? Not been here long?"

Mrs Raeburn frowned.

"I don't think I know her."

"But you must!" Miranda insisted. "Just came here recently. She said so herself."

"I'm sorry." Mrs Raeburn looked puzzled. "You

must have got it wrong. There's been no one new in your year since September. No one new in the school at all, since Christmas. And certainly no new girls."

She turned back to her computer.

"Close the door on your way out, will you?"

Very slowly, Miranda closed the door.

The Sponsored Walk went ahead, and it only rained for half the day. Miranda's ankle had healed, and she raised thirty-eight pounds fifty for the children's hospital.

And Rosie even made her a thank-you card.

Miranda never saw the girl again.

Be very careful, if you ever do. She could be anywhere. You might not know her, when you see her. But every time you face a decision about what's right… Every time you have to make a choice. She'll be there.

Watching.

Skip It!

Oliver stopped as he entered the yard at morning break.

A smile crossed his face.

Across the yard, some girls were skipping, using an old-fashioned long skipping rope with wooden handles. He could see Bethany, and Lina, Sarah, and other Sarah…

There was nothing unusual in that. Even in these days, girls still skipped.

What he didn't expect to see was his best mate, Harvey, joining in.

Oliver enjoyed the moment. Very quietly, he crept across to where they were all standing. Bethany had one end of the rope, and Sarah – other Sarah – the other.

The girls began to chant, an old skipping rhyme, as Harvey started to skip.

He skipped once, twice, three times…

"Boo!" Oliver shouted.

Harvey fell in a heap.

He glared upwards at Oliver from the hard ground.

"Oliver!" Lina glared. "You idiot!" She went to Harvey's aid. "Are you OK?"

Oliver had underestimated the impact of five girls

glaring at him. He determined to play it cool.

"Sorry if I'm interrupting." He grinned at Harvey. "Didn't want to interrupt all you little girls when you were playing."

"What's the matter, Oliver?" Gail strode forward, a tall and lanky presence with a mass of chestnut brown hair. She smirked. "Don't you know how to skip, then?"

Oliver blinked quickly.

"'Course…. But -" He hesitated. "It's for girls -"

"He doesn't know!" Gail crowed.

The other girls took this up.

"'Least Harvey had a go."

"What's the matter, Ollie?"

"Scared you might not be as good as a girl?"

They were crowding in around him, and Oliver, rather to his surprise, found himself backing away.

"Let's see you, then," Gail demanded. She took one end of the skipping rope and gave the other handle to Lina. "Come on!"

Even Harvey was waiting.

The girls began to twirl the rope.

Blushing crimson, Oliver made a small and hesitant jump. Then another…

On the third jump, the rope wound around his legs, and he found himself heading to earth.

"AAH!" A crowd of laughing and jeering girls closed in, looking down on Oliver. Gail smiled sweetly.

"Girls - one. Boys - nil."

"That was so embarrassing," Oliver told Harvey

later that day. They were strolling across the yard after lunch. "What were you doing it for, anyway?"

"It's fun." Harvey shrugged. "And it's good exercise. I can skip if I want to. After all, boxers skip, in training."

They stopped as they saw Gail and her friends. The girls had the skipping rope again, and Bethany's younger sister and her friend had joined them.

Oliver scowled.

"I'm not letting her get away with it, though."

He strode across to the girls, followed by Harvey.

"Oh, hello." Gail spoke the words less as a greeting than as a challenge. Her audience was sniggering. "It's the school athletics champion. Come to do some more skipping, Oliver?"

"There's not much time…" As a good friend, Harvey always knew when to come to the rescue. He glanced at his watch. "It's Science, in a minute."

"Plenty of time." Gail didn't let her victims go as easily as that. "Come on then, Ollie boy."

She grasped the end of the skipping rope.

"Round two."

With a look of grim determination, Oliver prepared himself.

"You don't *have* to do this," Harvey reminded him mildly.

Oliver ignored him.

"And an afternoon of Science coming up," he muttered.

Gail began to twirl the rope.

"I know one thing," Oliver said.

He stepped forward to take his first skip.

"There's one thing I'd like to skip. And that's Science lessons -"

Oliver's feet hit the ground.

He blinked.

There was no sign of Gail. Or the other girls. Or the yard.

He found himself standing at the front of the school, walking up the path towards the gate.

The gate was open, and through it poured a happy surge of chattering children and hassled-looking parents.

He looked at his watch.

Three-twenty.

It was the end of the day.

He turned to see Harvey by his side.

Like Oliver, Harvey was wearing his coat and carrying his bag. Like everyone else, he was obviously leaving school.

"Harvey?" Oliver gaped. "But I mean – like -"

He stared around him in bewilderment.

"What happened to the afternoon?"

"But it *did* happen," Oliver insisted. They were halfway up Station Road. "I was skipping – I said I wished I could skip the afternoon in school, you know, and Science, and then -"

He caught a glimpse, up a side road, of Gail and her friend Megan, walking home.

Oliver turned off towards them. He broke into a run.

"I'm gonna have some more of this!"

"You gone potty?" Gail asked, politely.

"Oh, come on, Gail!" Oliver pinkened slightly. He was embarrassed at the way Gail was looking at him, at Megan gawping.

But he had to do this.

"Just let me buy it off you."

Gail paused. Then she produced the skipping rope from her bag.

Oliver reached for it. But Gail held it above her head, using her height to the full.

"How much?"

Oliver quickly searched his pockets.

"Three pound fifty. A chewing gum wrapper – well, it could be worth twenty grand, it says so. You'll have to win the competition first…"

Gail hooted.

"You'll have to do better than that!"

"A purple pen." Oliver moved to his bag, handing items over recklessly. "A werewolf pencil sharpener -"

"Oi!" Harvey howled. "That's mine! I lent it you!"

Oliver ignored him.

"And…" He reached right down into the bag. "Two fast food vouchers. Look, you can get a triple burger, one of a wide selection of drinks, and fries."

Gail's eyes narrowed.

"Small or large?"

"Large," said Oliver quickly.

Gail paused.

"OK."

She handed the skipping rope over. There was a malicious look in her eyes as she took possession of all Oliver's treasures.

"Wait 'til I tell the others! That Oliver gave me all his stuff, just so he could go on playing with some mouldy old rope my sister threw out years ago…"

A grin spread across her face.

"*Now* who's the girl?"

With shrieks of laughter, she and Megan ran for the corner. They disappeared from view.

Harvey stood with a look of thoughtful sorrow.

"Isn't she horrible?" He blinked. "And she's got my sharpener."

"Right." Oliver clasped the rope firmly. He ran back the way they had come. "Come on! My place! Then I'll tell you what we do next."

"Are you sure about this?" Harvey asked.

They were standing in Oliver's small back garden, in the late afternoon sun. There, Oliver had tied one end of the skipping rope to the frame of his little sister's swing. He handed the other end of the rope to Harvey.

"You wait." Oliver's face was red with excitement. "If this works the way I think it does – you and me will have no worries for the rest of our lives."

"Ollie!" Oliver's Mum's voice came from the house.

"Can you come in, now, please? It's time for the dentist's!"

Oliver grimaced.

"And I'm having a filling done. Right. That settles it."

He motioned to Harvey.

"Come on. Twirl."

After a moment's hesitation, Harvey began to rotate the rope, slowly at first, then faster and faster.

Oliver wanted to be ready this time. He moved away, like a fast bowler ready to take a run-up.

Then he ran for the rope, and jumped.

Oliver caught his breath as he felt himself come to earth.

It was the weirdest feeling. One minute you were in one place, at one time, and the next…

He heard the school bell ring.

He knew how this worked, now. He looked at his watch.

Eight fifty-five.

He and Harvey were standing in the yard again, with all the other pupils, lining up for morning school.

He checked his bag, which was over his shoulder.

The skipping rope was inside, bundled on top of his English book and his PE kit.

He turned. Harvey was looking cheerful.

"It's Art, this morning. We can finish off making that octopus."

"I did it!" Oliver whispered. "I skipped last night. Missed the dentist."

As he said the last word, Harvey looked suddenly puzzled… confused. Slightly unwell.

He swayed slightly as he looked at Oliver.

"No – we did, didn't we? We were in your – I can't -"

He put a hand to his head.

"I can't… remember yesterday evening…"

"That's 'cause it never happened," Oliver explained, once lessons were underway. He dipped a brush into the splodgy dark green paint they were using to make their sea creatures. "I skipped it. And I skipped having my tooth done."

He had a smile that was growing by the second.

"Just think. We don't need to do anything we don't want to, ever again. We can just skip on to the bits we like. Miss everything else. Dentist's, new shoes, stuff round the house… "

His eyes gleamed.

"We've got the life of our dreams."

"I'd rather have my sharpener back." Harvey was looking glum as he shaped newspaper into a shark. "I loved that werewolf."

Oliver wasn't listening.

"Then think of all the lessons we can miss. Maths. Science. We could even miss whole days -"

He stopped.

"Yes!"

"I don't understand!" Harvey rushed out of the school into the yard when morning break arrived. He was struggling to keep up with Oliver.

"Very simple." Oliver headed straight for the Infants' climbing frame. "I'm getting the hang of how this works, now."

He produced the skipping rope from his bag, and tied it to the frame.

"First time, I made a little skip forward. To the end of the day. Then after school, I made a longer one. Missed out the evening. Landed up this morning."

He held the rope out to full length before handing the other end to Harvey.

"It's half-term next week. And what've I got, 'til then? History project. Sponsored silence on Thursday. And today we're on last dinners."

His mouth twisted into a smirk.

"This time… I want to skip a bit further. Saturday's the football match, and then out for pizza with you and Dad. The start of half-term. That'll do just fine."

He stared into Harvey's eyes.

"This time, I want you to spin it *really* fast."

"I still don't like it." Harvey was looking uncomfortable again. "I *wanted* last night. Mum was making chilli. Now I'll never get to eat it. *And* there was good stuff on TV."

"Ah, stop your moaning!" Oliver told him.

He pointed to the rope.

"Twirl."

Harvey paused. He gave Oliver a last, sad look.

Then he obeyed.

Oliver wasn't taking any chances. He took a long

run-up. He and Harvey were gathering a crowd. Other kids were staring, pointing. But he didn't care.

Harvey spun the rope, faster, and faster, and faster…

And Oliver ran forward, and jumped.

What happened next seemed to happen in slow motion. All Oliver remembered afterwards was Harvey's eyes, wide and horrified, and a strange feeling that the way down seemed much, much further than he had thought…

SLAM!

Oliver woke up. And he knew, straight away, that something was wrong.

He felt… odd. Different. His neck hurt, and when he tried to move his arms, or legs, it took much, much more effort than he was used to.

He was in hospital, that was it. He'd fallen after making his jump, hurt himself, and he was in hospital.

No. That was wrong. He wasn't lying in a bed, or on a trolley, as he would have been in hospital. He was in a sitting position. In what felt… like an old… rough, worn-out armchair. And there was a strange, nasty smell… like old, damp walls mixed with yesterday's school dinners.

He blinked, as his vision swam back into focus, trying to make out objects before him.

There was a fireplace on a wall of faded dark green paper. A battered old TV set…

And there was a person. A grown-up. Standing over him.

It was somebody old. A woman. He could see masses of grey hair, cascading down to her shoulders. She was tall, though stooped with age, and wore a faded blue and white checked dress. Quite like a school dress…

He squinted, as he came back to full consciousness, trying to make out the face…

Oliver gave a yell. He tried to leap up from the chair – and couldn't. His back hurt.

He could hardly move.

"So you're awake at last, are you?" the old woman said sharply. "About time. Home help will be here in a minute."

Oliver gasped for breath. It was several moments before he could say anything at all.

Finally, he managed:

"G-*Gail*?"

"You remember my name, then," the old woman said sourly. "Glad you've not gone completely senile. After all, we've only been married fifty-eight years."

Very slowly, Oliver forced himself out of the chair.

Moving, just moving about normally, felt so, *so* difficult…

And his voice had sounded odd, too – hoarser, weaker…

He caught sight of something on the wall above the fireplace.

A mirror.

He took a slow, hesitant step towards it. Then another…

His eyes widened at what he saw.

It was his face, he could just see that. His eyes, narrow and tired. His mouth, old and worried, in the middle of a maze of wrinkles.

And all his hair was gone.

The face that looked back at him was that of an old man.

"It's too late to worry about your appearance," Gail said. "Nothing you can do about it now, anyway."

"Gail?" Oliver turned back from the mirror. He forced himself to look again at Gail. She looked even worse, the second time... her skin was yellowy... and she had even more wrinkles than him.

Gail sniffed.

"So much for life. Seems to have been over in no time. I really backed a loser with you, didn't I?" She paused. For a moment, her eyes looked sad. "You know, sometimes I can't remember a single thing we ever did together."

"Gail?" Oliver gulped. He cringed at the sound of his old, creaky voice. "You mean... we're *married*?"

"Oh, dear." Gail rolled her eyes. "I'll have to get your medication changed."

Oliver heard a doorbell ring.

"Come on," Gail said wearily. "That'll be Glenda. Now remember, this time. Be nice to her."

She headed across to a door.

"She can make you some soup. You needn't think *I'm* cooking lunch for you."

"Hello, Oliver!" A plump and jolly young lady stepped into the room ahead of Gail.

Oliver had sunk back into the armchair, exhausted.

The young lady – Glenda, he supposed – beamed down at him. She spoke in a loud, bright, clear voice, at an oddly slow speed.

"How are we today, Oliver? Lovely day out there, isn't it?" She rearranged a cushion behind Oliver's head. "Now, are we going to make you some nice soup? What would you like today?"

"He'll have oxtail," Gail said. "That's all we've got, anyway. And some bread. The cheese went off."

"Lovely…" smiled Glenda. "Now, shall we have the telly on – eh?"

She went across to the TV.

"What'll it be, then? There might be a nice antique show on – or something about gardening?"

She turned to see an empty chair.

Oliver was gone.

Staggering, struggling to walk, Oliver hobbled along the narrow hallway. The house was small, and dark, and dingy, with very little furniture. Everything was old, and battered. There was no happiness anywhere, no joy – and no life.

He opened a door. It led to a tiny front room. There was a shabby sofa, the cushions splitting in places, their stuffing spilling out onto a worn and stained grey carpet.

Oliver caught sight of a table, with some cheap

photograph frames on display. He picked one up, looked at it. He looked at another.

The frames were empty. There must have been a dozen frames there – and no photographs.

Black, empty spaces stared back at him from where memories should have been.

He stumbled across to a bookcase, where all the shelves were filled with diaries. They started at the year he had been at school with Gail – and covered over seventy years since. He picked one out and opened it.

The pages were blank.

He flicked through another volume, then another.

And then he realised.

Nothing was there. Because nothing had happened, since that jump, that far-off day at school.

Nothing had ever happened to him, from that day to this.

He started to shake. The book fell from his hand, crashing to the floor.

"Your soup's ready," Gail said behind him.

Dazedly, he turned to face her.

Gail noted the diary on the floor.

"So much for life," she said bitterly. "Still, I suppose we should be happy, while we can. I suppose we'll be gone forever, soon. Like Harvey."

Oliver staggered, and almost fell.

"*Harvey*?" His eyes bulged. "You mean – Harvey's -"

"Oh, dear goodness." Gail closed her eyes, as if in pain. "We went to the funeral. Didn't we?"

She reached into her pocket.

"That reminds me. What was *this* doing by your bed?"

Oliver looked at the tiny black plastic object she held. Dumbly, he took it.

It was Harvey's sharpener.

Tears sprang to Oliver's eyes.

With a sudden burst of energy, he ran from the room.

"Hello, Oliver!" Glenda was smilingly transferring soup from a saucepan to a bowl as Oliver entered the poky and grubby kitchen. "It's just ready. It's – oh, where are you going?"

Oliver made no reply.

He opened a back door, stumbled out of the house.

It had to be somewhere. Where could it be?

The house had little garden. A small and scrappy piece of lawn, and a few dying shrubs.

But there was a tiny, dirty shed…

Oliver wrenched open its door. He rummaged through empty cardboard boxes… odd bits of wood… where was it?

"I'm getting worried about you," Gail said in the doorway. "And your soup's getting cold."

"Gail!" Oliver cried. "Where's the rope?"

"What?" Gail asked.

"Your skipping rope!" Oliver went on. "The one I bought off you, yesterday – I mean, when we were kids. Where is it?"

"Bit old for that, now, aren't you?" Gail asked.

She reached behind the boxes.

"Is this what you're looking for?"

Oliver made a grab for the rope. With sudden hope, he tied one end to the door handle, making sure it was secure.

"Quick!" He gave the other end of the rope to Gail. "Twirl it! And this time, it's got to be the other way."

The look on Gail's face showed she thought he had finally gone mad.

"I'll do nothing of the kind. What's got into you? You were bad enough at skipping when we were kids, as I recall. When we first met…"

All at once, she looked bewildered. And frightened.

"What happened after that?"

"Are you ready, Oliver?" Glenda had emerged into the garden. "What are you up to?"

"You!" Oliver grabbed the rope from Gail and flung it at Glenda. "Twirl the rope! Anticlockwise! Now!"

Such was the authority in his voice that a baffled Glenda obeyed.

"Oh, not you as well!" Gail shook her head. "Honestly, I think I'd better get the doctor here."

"Twirl!" Oliver shouted. "Now!"

Slowly and painfully, he stepped backwards, taking as long a run-up as he could manage.

"Oliver?" Still spinning the rope, Glenda blinked. "I'm not sure this quite fits with your care plan…"

"Oliver!" Gail yelled. "What are you doing?"

Glenda was already about to lower the rope. Gail was moving forward, wrinkled hands coming out to stop him…

"Putting things right!" Oliver shouted. "I hope! Giving us back our lives!"

He took a couple more steps backwards.

"And giving back Harvey his!"

In great pain, he took a run forward, and jumped.

SLAM!

"Ow." Oliver picked himself up, and rubbed his neck.

"Oliver?" Harvey blinked down at him, concerned. "You OK?"

"What were you playing at, Oliver?" On playground duty, Mrs Charles was looking annoyed. "That climbing frame is for the Infant classes! Not for Juniors to play silly tricks."

Oliver had never thought he would be so pleased to hear a teacher's voice.

"You'd better see Mr Gillespie," Mrs Charles finished, having made sure Oliver was all right. "At the end of break. And no skipping off."

She bent down and untied the rope from the frame.

"I'm confiscating this."

She walked away, leaving a crowd of grinning kids.

Oliver smiled at Harvey, a little painfully. His arm hurt, as well as his neck. So did his side.

He felt in his pocket.

Had he…?

"Here's your sharpener back." He threw it to Harvey, marvelling at how easy it suddenly was to throw. And walk. And run…

"Ah, cool!" Harvey caught the werewolf happily, and pocketed it.

"And I'll never be mean to you any more," Oliver went on emotionally. "And also, remind me never to have soup again."

"You sure you're OK?" Harvey started to make a careful examination of Oliver's head.

"Lost my rope already, have you?" Gail appeared. "And where's that sharpener gone? Oh. I see you've pinched it back."

She was back to being a girl, and her hair was brown.

"Typical boys. Still."

She smirked.

"I enjoyed those burgers."

"And," Oliver told her. "I'm never going to marry *you*, either."

With Harvey by his side, he walked away, leaving Gail gaping.

Only a Story

"I am a monkey," Simon told his class, "in the zoo."

There were stares of amazement, and some sniggering.

Simon swallowed.

"You're looking at me," he went on slowly. "But I'm looking at you."

He paused for breath, and looked nervously around the room. Jordon was grinning. Dean was smirking. Only Mrs Cole, whom he could just see out of the corner of his eye, was looking encouraging.

Simon held up the scrappy bit of file paper close to his face, using it like a shield.

He went on reading.

Sometimes I think I would like to be free
And swing through the jungle, from tree to tree

He could feel himself going red. He took a deep breath, and prepared for the worst.

But at least, while I'm here, I'm safe and well fed
And a nice pile of straw makes a warm, cosy bed.

There was a very long silence. Simon swallowed.

It wasn't the best poem he'd ever written. It was only six lines long, and his ideas, that afternoon, had been flowing like treacle.

And Simon had always been the writer of the class. He had a reputation to uphold.

"That's very good, Simon," said Mrs Cole. She looked at the class. "Wasn't that good?"

There were a few embarrassed mutters, and another snigger.

Mrs Cole looked back at Simon.

"I think you've really captured what it means to be a monkey."

"Well," muttered Jordon at the back. "He should know."

There were more sniggers.

"Now, then." Mrs Cole looked around for her next reader. Behind her was a display of several poems and stories the class had written.

She spotted the next poet in the queue.

"Dean."

Simon went and sat down, blushing crimson. From the other side of the room, Dean came swaggering, carrying his own poem. Dean's poem wasn't handwritten. It was word-processed, printed on high-quality computer paper, and looked more professional than Simon's effort, even before he started to read.

"Now, Dean," said Mrs Cole brightly.

Dean gave a brilliantly-timed dramatic pause before he began.

Tired of longing and tired of grieving
Tired of growing and never achieving
Tired when so little comes from believing
Tired of time, every stress and each strain.

There was a stunned silence. People were sitting up in their chairs. The girls had stopped trying to restyle each other's hair, the boys had stopped picking their noses or doodling on their books. Everyone was listening. Even Jordon.

Dean beamed triumphantly and went on.

Tired of wishing that I could still care
Tired when darkness ends days that seemed fair
Tired, with no joy and no kindness to spare
As time slips away and I set dreams aside.

Simon closed his eyes.

Dean continued.

Tired of the ignorance of those in authority
Tired, when the foolish make up the majority
While those who could change things remain the minority
Smiling politely while weeping inside.

He lowered his piece of paper.

There was a hush.

Then several of the class applauded.

"Well *done*, Dean," Mrs Cole gushed.

She picked up a small, yellow badge from her desk.

"Well," she told the class. "It's time to vote again. For Poet of the Week. All those who think Dean should win the badge?"

Practically everyone put their hand up. Except Simon.

"All those for Natalie's... *interesting* poem about her father's rats?"

Natalie and two of her friends cast their votes gigglingly.

"And all those for Simon?"

Simon put his hand up. No one else did.

Then everyone laughed.

Simon shrank down into his chair.

"Well, that seems like a clear majority." Mrs Cole turned to Dean, who still stood beside her. She presented the badge to him. "Congratulations, Dean. That's Poet of the Week, third week running."

It was half an hour later. Almost hometime. Simon had never been so pleased to see the end of the day.

Then, five minutes before the final bell, Mrs Cole made the announcement.

"Before you all go, I have some exciting news."

The class didn't look enthusiastic. They all knew that "exciting news" meant either a sponsored swim or another visit from the Mayor.

"Our school," said Mrs Cole, "is going to hold a story-writing competition. It'll be judged by Mrs Raeburn, myself, and a local author."

At least some of the class were listening now.

"The winning pieces of fiction from each year group," Mrs Cole went on, "will go into a specially-printed, limited edition School Storybook, which will be available to our pupils and their families."

More people were now listening. Simon was looking interested. And so was Dean.

"And the winner overall," Mrs Cole finished. "Will receive a prize of twenty pounds. In the form of a book token."

Now, everyone was listening.

"That was dead funny," Dean told Simon on their way out. "You, standing there like a beetroot in a jumper, going: "I am a monkey in the zoo…""

"Shut up," Simon told his fellow artist coldly. There was a small crowd of other boys around Dean. No one was standing around Simon.

"Are you going to enter for that story competition, Dean?" Dimitrius asked.

"I'm not just going to enter." Dean straightened his tie smugly. "I'm going to win."

"No," said Simon loudly and suddenly. "*I* am."

"No," said Dean firmly. "I am."

"No, I am."

"What are you gonna write about?"

"I'm not telling you. What's your story?"

"I'm not telling you."

"Fine, then."

And Simon stormed off.

There was silence.

"He is so not gonna win," Dean reassured his followers. "I mean, I'm like well better at English."

Simon went straight from school to the children's library. He needed somewhere he could think.

It had been like this ever since Dean had come to the school. Poems. Stories. Haiku…

Of course, *Dean* was a published author. *Dean*'s parents had paid to have some of his poems printed. *Dean* had won a local newspaper competition for one of his short stories, and had his photo taken. Dean was a real writer.

Simon still hadn't got beyond the school magazine.

When Simon arrived at the library, there was more bad news.

He found Mrs Thwaite packing picture books into boxes. She was the Children's Librarian and he had known her for as long as he could remember.

He looked around. No one was sitting on the cushions in the Book Corner. No one was writing or drawing on the Story Board. No one was reading.

Even for a library, it was quiet.

"What's happening?" he asked.

Mrs Thwaite smiled sadly.

"It's happened at last." She moved quickly away from Simon to take down an alphabet chart from the wall. "Well. They've been threatening it long enough."

"What?" Simon demanded.

"The Council," Mrs Thwaite explained. "They're

closing us down. A local Children's Library isn't "cost effective" now. Whatever that may mean. So they're closing us down here and moving what's left over to the main library at Sansford Central."

She took a deep breath.

"And good luck to them. I'll be retiring, in August."

"No way…" Simon looked around the library area. Every corner had a memory. Storytellers in the school holidays when he was little… helping to feed the tropical fish in their blue glass tank… last summer, when the older kids had done their own puppet show for the younger ones and Simon had written the script. He could see two of the puppets now, a knight and a wicked witch, looking hopefully out of their battered cardboard box as if waiting to be part of another story.

Sansford Central was miles away…

He caught sight of a long trestle table. It was covered with the older books, with their faded and battered covers and thumbed and grubby pages.

A piece of paper fastened to the front of the table read: EVERYTHING HERE 20p OR 30p.

Mrs Thwaite saw where he was looking.

"We're getting rid of those. They've no need for them at Central." She brightened a little. "They're only twenty or thirty pence each. Perhaps you'd like to buy some, Simon. I'd like to know they're going to a good home."

Simon had a look through the books. Some, the library must have had for years.

He knew you could find out how old they were by

looking at the left-hand page in the front. He chose a book at random.

First published 1975. Published in paperback 1976. Reprinted 1977, 1979, 1983, 1988…

These were books you couldn't even buy any more.

He wondered how many children had read these books, over the decades. What they'd thought of them. And where all those children were, now.

He sorted through some more. Some, he had read. A few didn't look like anyone had read them for ages. The pages had gone yellow.

He chose sci-fi novels, a picture book he had always loved, a children's book of recipes. At least these few books would be safe, with him.

He was almost finished when he caught sight of something sticking out from beneath a huge illustrated poetry book.

He pulled the mystery item out.

It was a paperback, with a dark green cover. It was obviously one of the oldest books there. A look inside told him it had been published in 1968. There was no mention of a reprint.

But it was the beautiful picture of a dragon on the front that caught his eye. That, and the title.

The Land of Swaythe.

He looked at the contents page, quickly read the blurb on the back of the book. The book contained three tales, all set in the same magical fantasy world.

He read the opening lines of the first story.

Deep beneath the land of Swaythe, beyond the Woods and

hidden in the shadows of Mount Apex, there lived a dragon…

He jumped as he looked up to see Mrs Thwaite standing over him.

"There's quite a few here I'd like to buy."

"Good for you," Mrs Thwaite said. She held out a plastic ice cream tub to receive Simon's change.

"When…" Simon swallowed. "When do you actually…?"

"Just make sure you're here on the 11th," Mrs Thwaite answered. "The final Saturday. We're having a sort of farewell party. Storytellers, shadow puppets. Orange squash."

Her voice hardened.

"I want to make sure we don't just fade away. Whatever they may want."

Simon was cross with himself.

There was no homework that evening, and he'd meant to start work on a story for the competition. He had a wonderful idea for a fantasy story, a tale about an elf and his voyage across the seas to find his father.

But somehow, the words wouldn't come. The story was there, in his head, but he couldn't get the ideas from his head into his hand, into his pen or onto the page. He had a computer and word-processing software at home, but trying to type the story straight onto the screen met with no more success.

Whenever he closed his eyes, whenever he tried to let his imagination take flight, all he could see was Dean's smug, grinning face.

In the end, he gave up for the night. He would have to come up with something soon. There were only two weeks before the competition stories had to be in.

He lay on his bed, enjoying the silence and the gathering darkness outside the window, with just his bedside light on, surrounded by his hoard of old books. He spent a happy hour rediscovering them.

Downstairs, Mum and Dad had the TV on. They didn't know what they were missing.

The Land of Swaythe was the one that really grabbed him. They didn't write children's books like that any more. It was old-fashioned stuff, but exciting, and funny, and it tugged on his heartstrings a couple of times. It was all about a land ruled over by an evil sorceress, and there was a dragon, and three knights set off to rescue a princess…

After a while, he was completely caught up in its fantasy world. Somehow, being set in an older time made it harder to spot that it wasn't a modern book. Even if the cover was nearly coming off.

The first of the three tales was the best. Simon had always thought that beginnings were the most exciting.

He so wanted to be a fantasy author. If only he could come up with something like that first tale, for the competition…

Then he had the idea. And it was so terrible, and so much against the way he normally behaved, that he felt shocked.

He couldn't look at the book any more. He shoved it onto the top of his bookshelf, and pushed it out of sight, right to the back, placing other books in front.

He went to bed, soon afterwards. But the images of Dean's face, and of his own awful poetry reading in front of the class that day, stayed with him long into the night.

And so did the idea.

"I've started work on my story," Dean said next day, over their pasta bolognaise in the dining hall. "And. It's based on a true story. Which actually happened to my family."

At the end of the table, Simon sipped his water. He made no comment.

"It happened in the Second World War, yeah?" Dean went on. "My great-grandad lived on the coast. Somewhere up north. And they had a fortress there, guarding the coastline from the enemy. And one night, there was an air raid. And my great-grandad -"

He suddenly became aware that Simon was listening.

"Well, you'll have to wait and see."

"Sounds good," Elliott said. The other boys agreed.

"We're going up there especially, this weekend," Dean went on. "So I can see the place. You've got to get proper inspiration. When you're a writer."

His voice rose. He was talking to the whole table now.

"And Dad's taking me to the War Museum too. So I can research."

He gave Simon a sly look.

"Are you gonna be researching, too? Spending the weekend in the zoo, with your friends, the monkeys?"

A laugh was passed from one boy to another, down the length of the table. It landed on Simon when it got to the end.

Furiously, Simon bit into his flapjack.

Simon wiped the sweat from his brow with the back of his hand.

He was sitting at home once more, in front of his computer, and panicking.

The two weeks were up. The competition entries had to be in by lunchtime tomorrow.

And Simon hadn't written a word.

Nothing had worked. The elf story had failed. None of his other ideas had come to anything. He had spent two weeks typing and deleting words. And now his screen and his mind were completely blank.

What was worst of all was that the nasty idea hadn't gone away. It was still there, deep in his head, whispering all the time in his ear that it didn't have to be like this, no one could ever know, he could show Dean once and for all just who was the best…

No. He wasn't going to do it. If he couldn't win honestly… then too bad. He knew he was a good writer. Dean didn't matter. No one else mattered…

His phone beeped. He opened the text message.

His eyes bulged.

How you doin mate? I handed my story in 2day. Nothin

from u yet? Having trubble? Take my tip mate. Leave it to the real writers lol!!!

It was signed. *Dean.*

He didn't know who had given Dean his mobile number.

That was it for Simon. He leapt to his feet.

He looked at the clock. 8.30pm. He probably just had time…

With sudden firmness, he strode over to the bookshelf, grabbed *The Land of Swaythe* and opened it at the first tale.

Then he sat down at the computer again and furiously started to type.

Deep beneath the land of Swaythe, beyond the Woods and hidden in the shadows of Mount Apex, there lived a dragon…

"Miss," said Simon, as the class left for lunch the next day. His mouth felt dry. He had been waiting all morning to do this, putting it off.

Very nervously, he produced a plastic wallet containing a few printed A4 pages.

"I've done my story. For the competition."

His hand shook slightly as he held the folder out. His voice sounded slightly squeaky.

He felt as if he'd stolen something.

He had.

"Ah!" Mrs Cole took the folder smilingly. "I was wondering what had happened to yours. Not like you to leave things 'til the last minute, Simon."

She slid the pages out of the folder and started to read. Simon was longing to turn and run, but she motioned to him to wait.

A very long fifteen seconds followed.

Then Mrs Cole's eyes met his.

There was another agonising second before she spoke.

"Simon. This is simply wonderful."

Simon smiled a ghastly smile.

Mrs Cole took another look at the pages.

"For someone your age… it's really quite incredible."

Simon tried to look proud.

"Of course," Mrs Cole went on. "I know where it came from."

The room spun. Simon staggered.

Finally, he managed to speak.

"D-do you, miss?"

Mrs Cole smiled.

"It came from all that extra effort you've been putting into your writing. Those Creative Writing workshops… and the Writer in Residence I brought in. I'm so pleased to see at least some of my students trying to improve their level of English."

Quickly, she put the pages back into their folder.

"I'd better not say any more now. The competition still has to be judged. And you're just in time."

She glanced again at the title.

"*The Land of Swaythe* will go into the competition along with the other entries."

She paused.

Simon wasn't moving. He seemed to be in suspended animation.

"Well, off you go then," Mrs Cole laughed. "It's lunchtime!"

Simon blinked.

Very shakily, he headed for the door.

Simon heard no more about the competition that day, or the next. Dean was being his usual annoying self. But even he had stopped talking about the story he had written.

Then, on Friday afternoon, the bombshell came.

"All right, quiet everyone!" Mrs Cole called, as the school day was drawing to a close. "I've got a special announcement to make! It's about the School Storybook competition. As they say on those awful TV shows you all watch, the results are in."

For once, everyone stopped and listened.

"We now have a winner for this class. Who is also the winner for this year group."

Dean sat up very straight in his chair.

"I'm very proud to say," Mrs Cole went on, "that more than one of the contenders for this year group came from this class. We had Jordon's… *unusual* tale of a boy known only as Mr J, who by sheer brute force becomes ruler of the world…"

Jordon grinned.

"But," Mrs Cole went on, "from what I've heard, the one everyone seems to be talking about is Dean's account of the Second World War, *Flight Over The Fort*."

Dean smirked.

Mrs Cole held up the folder containing Dean's work.

"Dean, this is a very good piece of writing, it's well-researched, well-written and gives a very vivid telling of what happened that night in 1941."

There was a pause, during which Dean's head seemed to be getting ever bigger.

"Unfortunately," Mrs Cole said, "I'm afraid it had to be disqualified."

Never had the classroom been so quiet. Simon's eyes widened. Dean looked as if he'd been hit with a sledgehammer.

"You see, Dean," Mrs Cole explained. "This is a *true* story. And I explained quite clearly that this was a competition for writing fiction. Your story had to be entirely made up. What you've given me here is effectively a factual account."

It was the first time anyone had seen Dean lost for words.

Mrs Cole smiled sympathetically.

"Never mind, Dean. Your writing's coming along splendidly. Perhaps you could use this when you study World War Two next term."

A grin spread across Simon's face as he saw Dean's expression.

Then the grin dropped off, as Mrs Cole picked up another sheaf of papers from her desk.

"But the winner," Mrs Cole announced, "for the

whole of our year group, and going into the School Storybook, is a quite excellent fantasy story about a dragon and knights and sorcery, *The Land of Swaythe*. By our very own author, Simon!"

There was a small buzz of excitement, and even some applause.

Mrs Cole beamed.

"Come forward, Simon."

Weakly, Simon staggered forward.

The class was looking at him with a new respect.

But he wasn't enjoying it, at all.

Simon spent a cold and confused weekend of sleepless nights, unfinished meals and Mum and Dad asking him if he felt all right. He had the thermometer shoved into his mouth twice on Sunday afternoon alone.

"Is someone bullying you?" Mum asked.

Simon shook his head.

"I don't know what's the matter with you," Mum went on. "You've won the writing thing, for the whole of your year! I thought you'd be pleased. Everyone was talking about it to me at PTA. I've ordered ten copies of the School Storybook. We'll send one to your Auntie Clare, and one to Granny…" She smiled. "That was one in the eye for Dean's mother. Shows she's not the only one with a son who can write."

Simon said nothing.

His mood didn't improve on Monday morning when, after Assembly, Mrs Raeburn the Head sent for him. He knocked at her office door so quietly she didn't hear him, and he had to do it again.

He found Mrs Cole waiting for him in there, too.

"Simon." Mrs Raeburn smiled, to his relief. "I wanted to speak to you. Firstly, to congratulate you on having won the writing competition for your year…"

"Thank you, miss," said Simon in a mouse-sized voice.

Mrs Raeburn exchanged glances with Mrs Cole.

"And secondly…" Mrs Raeburn said slowly. "For having won first prize out of the entire school."

Simon gulped.

Mrs Raeburn picked up some sheets of paper from her desk. Simon could see they were photocopies of his story.

Not his story.

"This really is quite astonishing," Mrs Raeburn said. "Based on this, I really think you have an extraordinary talent. I'd like to speak to your parents about getting you onto one of the Gifted and Talented programmes… the Summer School…"

Simon's eyes popped.

"In the meantime," Mrs Raeburn went on, "and this is really why I've sent for you… I would like to invite you to read your story – to the whole school. On stage. During the Prize Giving at the end of term. And after that, our local author – who *loved* your story, incidentally – will present you with your book token."

There was silence.

"Well, Simon," said Mrs Cole, a little sharply.

"Aren't you going to thank Mrs Raeburn?"

"Thank you, miss," Simon whispered.

It was the final week of term.

And Simon found himself in the school Hall, sitting on stage, on a chair between the Lady Mayoress and Mr Gillespie the Deputy Head. There were potted plants aplenty, and a huge screen that was showing bold purple letters that read:

Celebrating all we have achieved.

Next to Mr Gillespie was another guest… a grey-haired lady that Simon didn't recognise.

All the kids were in the Hall already, and the parents were flocking in. The place was packed.

And Simon had never been so nervous in his life.

He could see Mum. He could see Mrs Cole, who was looking proud. He could see Dean, fuming as he looked up at Simon.

That was something, anyway.

"Everyone ready?" Mrs Raeburn came bustling onto the stage. "I think we've got that microphone fixed. Just be careful, please, everyone, if you have to say anything containing the letter P."

She smiled sickeningly at the guests, then turned to Simon.

"Now, Simon. You know the order of things?"

He should have done. She'd been through it with him enough times.

"First, I'll open the proceedings," Mrs Raeburn explained, again, "and then the Lady Mayoress will speak. Then we'll have our local author, before she introduces you. Then – you're on! Remember, Simon. Big voice. Make sure they can hear you at the back. Best of luck. And well done, once again. All right?"

She made for the microphone.

"Good afternoon, ladies, gentlemen and children. And welcome to our annual Prize Giving."

Simon didn't hear a word that Mrs Raeburn or the Lady Mayoress said. His eyes moved from being fixed on the floor, to the other kids all looking up at him, to Mum, looking very superior and wearing a new coat, and back again.

In trembling hands he held the manuscript of *The Land of Swaythe*.

It was OK, he kept telling himself. The book hadn't been reprinted for years. It was obvious no one in the school had ever read it. This wouldn't go any further than the school competition. After today, it would all be over.

He wasn't so sure about the Summer School…

He woke up, suddenly. Mrs Raeburn was speaking again.

"Now, unfortunately, our local author who kindly gave his time to judge our competition is unable to be with us today. But in his place, and also from the world of authoring, we welcome a rather special guest, who has recently returned to this town, and in fact some years ago attended this very school.

'I'm sure we'd all like to extend a warm welcome to Mrs Barnstaple."

The grey-haired lady rose and stepped up to the microphone. She had a warm smile and sounded frightfully nice.

"Thank you," she said, a little shyly. "Thank you, Mrs Raeburn. It seems a long time ago – it *is* a very long time ago – that I was a pupil at this school, and sat in Assembly in this very Hall. I've lived most of the last forty years in Gloucestershire, actually, with my family. But one thing that links all of those days, all of those times together, is my love of writing. When I was here, English was my favourite subject. And I love to see just how much a good book means to young people. And how it inspires you to write, in your turn."

She glanced at Simon.

"Although I haven't yet had the chance to read this young man's work, I hear he is an author of great promise. I shall have to watch out!"

There was a ripple of laughter.

"But it was in this town," Mrs Barnstaple went on, "– and don't worry, I shan't bore you longer than I have to – that I myself turned to writing a children's book. Although I used a pen-name, and the book hasn't been in print for many years, it was inspired by some of our beautiful local countryside, and I'm pleased to say a local publishing house has recently agreed to reprint it. And I shall be donating some copies to your school library. And so, as a little tribute to those days I would just like, if I may, to read you a few lines of the story that first came into my head in this school, when I was your age."

She held up a book, with a new and shining cover.

"*The Land of Swaythe*!"

Never in history had a school Hall fallen so silent. Mrs Raeburn looked thunderstruck. Simon's Mum looked about to faint.

Simon himself was holding onto his chair for support.

Apparently not seeing any of this, Mrs Barnstaple began to read in a slow, wavering voice.

"*Deep beneath the land of Swaythe, beyond the Woods and hidden in the shadows of Mount Apex, there lived a dragon…*"

Mrs Raeburn turned to look at Simon.

But Simon was no longer there.

As a writer, he knew when a story wasn't going to have a happy ending.

Christmas Shopping

"There's no doubt about it," Liam proclaimed. "The guy who invented these places is a genius."

He and Justin stood together at the entrance to the store. Cheap silver Christmas trees stood in the window display, and red tinsel and stars lined the walls in honour of the festive season. A pile of brightly-labelled cleaning products stood to their left, and a stack of boxes of chocolates and sweets lay to their right.

Above Justin's head, a huge red and green sign read: "EVERYTHING IN THIS SECTION £1 OR LESS".

"I mean," Liam went on, "where else could you do all your Christmas shopping in one store?"

Carefully, he took from his pocket a crisp £10 note. He unfolded it lovingly. "Ten quid here, from Mum, to buy Christmas presents. That's a pound for hers. A pound for Dad's. And I guess…a pound for big sister."

He allowed a satisfied grin to spread across his face.

"And that leaves… seven quid for me."

Justin was frowning over his own funds. A heap of fifty and twenty pence pieces lay in the palm of his hand.

Liam gave them a glance.

"You been playing on the fruit machines again?"

"I've got to do the whole family for this," Justin told him. He gave Liam a baleful look. "*And* I saved it up myself."

Liam wasn't even listening. He was making for the section with the sign that read: "GIFTS". Justin grabbed a wire shopping basket from the stack next to the entrance, and followed him.

Liam picked up some bubble bath.

"There's big sister sorted." He glanced at his wristwatch. "In under twenty seconds." He looked around. "Now…"

They moved deeper into the store, past brightly-coloured soft toys and plastic water pistols.

"Come on then." Liam turned to his friend for help. "Something for Mum, something for Dad."

"How about them?" Justin pointed upwards. "Them biscuits look OK."

Liam took one look.

"They're dog biscuits, you twit!" He looked around. Suddenly, there was pet food all around them. "How big is this place?" They already seemed to be miles from the door.

"There's more stuff near the back." Justin picked up a bone-shaped dog toy and gave it an experimental squeak.

Liam had spotted something…some socks and ties, on display in the far corner. "Ah, here's the Dad Department."

He picked out a particularly dazzling tie in scarlet and gold.

"He can wear that when he's meeting important business clients."

"He's a plumber, isn't he?" Justin frowned.

"Contractor," Liam corrected him coldly. "Plumbing, heating and drainage services. You've seen the van." He placed the tie into the basket with the bubble bath. "He can wear it at weddings."

"These aren't bad." Justin was poking around in another of the displays, a revolving stand of cheap pieces of jewellery mounted on cardboard. He picked out a necklace, made to look like gold, with a heart-shaped pendant.

"I'll get you one for Christmas," Liam sniggered.

"Not for me!" Justin put the necklace into the basket. "For my sister. Stop her being jealous. I'm getting the real thing for my Christmas present. Signet ring."

"That's cool." Liam nodded approvingly.

They moved down an aisle filled with CDs of bands and singers they had never heard of.

"I missed all the Christmas stuff at school." Justin was looking glum. "You wait all year to get a cold. And then it comes at Christmas-time." He turned to Liam. "What did you do?"

Liam shrugged.

"All the usual stuff. Santa for the little kids. Disco for us. There was a Christmas carol concert, and a Christmas dinner. Turkey roll and mince pies."

"Salty gravy and sprouts," Justin remembered. He looked doleful. "Now I'll have to wait a whole year to eat that again."

"Sprouts." Liam wrinkled up his nose. "I'm glad I wasn't sitting next to you in class, that afternoon." He grinned. "I tell you something I heard at the school disco, though. You'll have to watch yourself. Watch out for Lydia and Chelsea."

"The twins?" Justin frowned. "Why?"

Liam smirked.

"One of them wants to go out with you."

"*What?*" Justin looked alarmed. "Which one?"

"Not sure," Liam admitted. "One sister told me that the other one... I forget which way round it was. Either way, it's double trouble. I went to their Christmas party at their house last year."

"*I'm* going this year!" Justin sounded really worried now. "Day after Boxing Day."

"You might want to get out of that, mate," Liam advised. He grinned once more. "Tell 'em you're ill. Say it was your Mum's sprouts that did it."

They had passed on into the household goods.

"And there..." Liam made a lunge for the kitchen utensils, "is Mum." He grabbed an egg whisk, the first thing that came to hand. "Well, she said she wanted to find time to cook more." He laughed. "We're going to a restaurant for our Christmas lunch."

Justin took out the handful of coins again from his pocket. He headed back towards the front of the store.

"I think I'll just get chocolates for Mum and Dad. Lewis likes these, too." He picked up a box. "And so do I."

"Three presents in one." Liam sounded impressed.

"Wish I'd thought of that. Never mind, we're done now. Don't need paper. Get some fancy bows from the Post Office, for a few p, 'cause my Mum likes 'em. Three nice Christmas presents. Sorted."

"And the rest," Liam said, "is mine."

He emerged from the confectioners, staggering under the weight of the biggest tin of sweets Justin had ever seen.

"Wow." Justin examined the tin with the eye of an expert. "Hey, aren't these the ones with the caramel centres?"

He was already picking at the tape sealing the lid.

"Hey, get off 'em, will you?" Liam shoved Justin's hand away. "That was *my* seven quid, wasn't it?"

He grinned.

"Tell you what. Carry 'em for me, 'til we've finished. And I'll let you have some, when you come over on Boxing Day. *If* I've got any left."

Justin gave Liam a look. He took the tin, nonetheless.

They walked through the precinct. It was late afternoon, and the Christmas lights were on. Grandmothers were shopping for their grandchildren's Christmas presents. Hassled-looking Mums pushed buggies and struggled with carrier bags. Three other kids hung around outside the burger bar, laughing. There was the smell of candy-floss and doughnuts from a street trader's stall.

They could sense the season in the air.

They reached the bus stop just as the bus was

pulling in. There, they parted, Justin to head home, Liam to go to tea at his Gran's a few streets away.

"See you on Boxing Day, then," Justin said. "Merry Christmas, mate."

"Have a good one," Liam answered. "Don't eat too many mince pies."

The bus drew away, Justin giving a quick wave.

Liam stood watching for a moment, alone.

Then he realised.

"Oi!" he shouted. "You've still got my sweets!"

The bus disappeared around the corner.

My World

The door to the small spare bedroom opened slightly.

Joe's round, freckled face peeped out.

He made sure the coast was clear. He crept along the landing and peered over the banister rail.

The house was quiet. It was a dark early January day, and only the lights of the Christmas tree lit the hall. Somewhere distant, a TV was on.

Christmas was over now. Soon, Joe would be going home.

He scurried along to the room of his cousin, Lucy. He tried the door.

It was locked.

Joe banged on it as hard as he could.

"Lucy? You in there?"

"Go away!" Lucy's voice came back with all the superiority of being four years older than Joe. "I'm busy." A pause. "I thought you were meant to be ill?"

"I'm better now." Joe put on his sweet voice, the one he used when he wanted everyone to feel sorry for him. "They're all still cross with me down there. 'Cause we couldn't go to the pantomime."

"It was *your* fault you were sick," Lucy's voice came back in a motherly tone. "Eating all that chocolate. *And* before breakfast."

"It was only half a selection box!" Joe protested.

"*My* selection box," Lucy pointed out. "I was saving that."

"I didn't want it to go to waste," Joe pointed out, reasonably. "You're not still meant to have any chocolate left, at New Year. I think it's against the law."

He frowned.

"What you doing in there?"

"I told you," Lucy answered. "I'm busy."

"That's not an answer," Joe pointed out. "You should say: "I'm washing my hair", or "I'm reading about rabbits", or "I'm watching TV"…"

"Or…" Lucy suggested, ""I'm trying to stop my bratty little cousin from being nosey.""

Joe stuck his tongue out at the closed door.

"I saw that," Lucy called. Joe jumped.

There was a silence.

But Joe wasn't beaten yet.

"Anyway," he said, more quietly. "Whatever you're doing, it's not *half* as interesting as what's going on out here."

There was a pause before Lucy answered.

"What?"

"You'd be surprised," Joe answered. "Still." He managed to shrug, through his voice alone. "You want to miss it…"

Another pause.

Then the door was unlocked from the inside. It opened, just a tiny crack.

Lucy's face appeared.

And in that second, Joe pushed past her and into the room.

"Oh, you little -" Lucy screamed. "I *knew* you were making it up!"

"Had to look though, didn't you?" Joe grinned.

He skidded to a halt.

"Whoa."

He blinked. Lucy had never allowed him into her room before.

"So this is what you hide in here."

The little room was crammed with books and files and papers. The whole of the far wall was lined with bookshelves, almost up to the ceiling. There were storybooks, picture books, children's books about science and history and the environment. Everything Lucy had ever read must have been there.

On the opposite wall were more shelves, packed with cardboard folders and transparent plastic wallets.

And on Lucy's small desk was page after page of A4 paper, piled high, some spilling over onto the floor.

Every page was covered with words, all written in Lucy's neat, sloping handwriting in bright purple ink. She had used every scrap of space on every piece of paper.

"What are you writing?" Joe was at the desk in under five seconds. He picked up a page. "And what's Sandyways?"

Lucy grabbed the page back off him.

"Never you mind."

"There's more over here." Joe poked about among the plastic folders on the nearest shelf. He could see more purple-covered pages. "How long have you been writing this stuff?"

"Quite a while," Lucy answered. She no longer looked cross. She looked excited, and her eyes shone. "Actually, three years, seven months." She blinked. "Since I was about your age."

""The sun was shining in Sandyways that afternoon,"" Joe read from another page he'd picked up without asking, ""as Lucy walked along the seafront.""

He turned back to Lucy.

"What is it?"

With great dignity, Lucy took the page from him. She placed it carefully back onto the desk.

"If you must know, Sandyways is my world."

"You mean," Joe asked, "it's like, a story?"

"More than that." Lucy fixed her eyes on him, wide and serious. "It's a real place I created. I write more about it every day. I've never missed a day, even when I was on holiday. Even when I had the chicken pox. These -"

She moved her arm to indicate the folders.

"These contain Sandyways' history for the last three and a half years."

She stared dreamily at the pages on the desk.

"You're the first one I've ever told."

"You've never shown it to anyone else?" Joe asked.

Lucy shook her head.

"It's *my* world."

Joe's face wore a curious look.

"Can you take other people there?"

Lucy shrugged.

"I don't know. Maybe. If I wanted to."

"Can I come?" Joe asked.

"No," Lucy said.

"Aw!" Joe put on his most sympathetic look. "Why not?"

"You don't understand," Lucy went on. She looked at the shelves again. "It's my world. My people. The people of Sandyways depend on me. I solve all their problems for them. Like last winter, when it snowed, and we had to get the snowplough out to rescue everyone who'd got stranded. And when invaders came, we had to repel the attack, from the Castle. I ended up taking charge of the army myself." She smiled. "But we saved the town from the enemy."

"Sounds exciting," Joe said.

"There are quieter days too, of course," Lucy continued. She smiled. "Sometimes, after school, I just like to go and stroll along the beach, and have tea at Mrs Rafferty's – she runs the tea shop on the Parade. On a cold day like this in our world, it can be hot and sunny in Sandyways, like it is today. It can be summer or winter. Exciting, or happy and relaxing. Whatever we like."

"Hang on." Joe gave her a crafty look. "Did you just say "we"?"

Lucy looked at him.

"I suppose," she muttered, half to herself, "it would be nice to show it all to someone. That's if it works. It should do…"

She stared straight into Joe's eyes.

"Joe. If I take you. Will you promise to be good? Do exactly what I tell you?"

"Yeah!" Joe answered eagerly. "Sure!"

"It's *my* world," Lucy warned. "My people. And my rules."

Joe shrugged.

"OK."

Lucy looked doubtful for a moment.

Then she turned back to the desk. She beckoned to Joe.

"Come here."

Joe stepped up to the desk.

Lucy took a new sheet of paper. She picked up her pen and started to write.

"*The sun was shining in Sandyways that afternoon,*" Lucy read what she was writing, "*as Lucy…*" She stopped, and added in a name. "*As Lucy and Joe walked along the seafront…*"

Joe gave a yell.

Lucy's bedroom had disappeared.

All at once, they were in the open air.

Gorgeous sunshine beamed down from a cloudless sky. A mild breeze was blowing.

To their left was a row of tall, white, graceful

buildings, shops and cafes and elegant houses. To their right were railings, with a flight of steps leading down to a golden, sandy beach.

There was no litter. No traffic. And everything was beautifully still.

"No chilly mornings here." Lucy took Joe's hand, and Joe was too amazed to refuse. "No end of the Christmas holidays, and no going back to school. It's my world. We're safe here. And happy. For as long as we like."

Joe blinked.

"Where are all the people?"

Lucy shrugged.

"You can have people if you like."

The next moment, there were people everywhere. Couples walked along the beach, waiters and waitresses brought trays to tables outside pavement cafes.

"Wow!" Joe grinned. "You're brilliant!"

Lucy smiled proudly.

"Of course," she went on. "I don't always have people. Sometimes, I do without them altogether."

She led Joe along the promenade.

"This is the Parade," she explained, like a tour guide. "And way over there…" She pointed, and Joe squinted to see the shape of distant towers. "That's the Castle."

She stopped, and smiled at Joe.

"Are you hungry?"

"Yes," Joe answered automatically.

"Come on then." Lucy led Joe away. "I'll take you to Mrs Rafferty's. For tea."

"You've not got any money, have you?" Joe asked.

"Don't need any, here," Lucy answered. "It's my world."

Joe followed her towards a small, old-fashioned tearoom.

A bell rang as Lucy opened the door. There were lace tablecloths, and brass ornaments, and somewhere, someone was making toast.

"I love it here," Lucy beamed.

She made for a table near the fireplace.

"I come here at least twice a week. And sometimes for lunch, at weekends."

"Wow!" As usual, Joe was somewhere else – somewhere he shouldn't have been. He pulled back a velvet curtain. Beyond, a high window looked onto a vast starscape. "It's outer space out here!"

"Yes," Lucy answered, rather sharply. "There's a portal here into space. It was a bad idea. I did it after we did astronomy at school. There are aliens and things out there…. We're not having that sort of adventure today."

All at once, the window and the curtain disappeared.

Joe looked disappointed.

"Come and sit down." Lucy smiled again. "There are lots of nice cakes."

Joe cheered up at once.

His mouth watered as he saw the large table next to Lucy's. There was a huge cream gateau topped with strawberries… a lemon cake, thickly iced… a plate of gooey chocolate éclairs…

"I can recommend the treacle tart," Lucy said. "With cream. Fresh, of course."

She turned as someone approached them, and smiled.

"Hello, Mrs Rafferty!"

"Hello, Lucy!" The voice belonged to a handsome, dark, comfortable-looking woman. She had a black shawl draped around her shoulders, and jangled with a lot of jewellery. "I'd hoped you might come in today. Kept the second treacle tart back for you, just in case."

"Thank you," Lucy beamed.

"And who's this?" Mrs Rafferty asked.

"Oh…" Lucy looked across the table. "This is my cousin Joe. He's just visiting."

"Hello, Joe." Mrs Rafferty gave Joe a warm smile. "Tea for two, then?"

"Please," Lucy answered. "And treacle tart for me." She looked to her cousin. "What would you like, Joe?"

"I've just the thing for you," Mrs Rafferty said to Joe. "Chocolate cake. Freshly baked this morning."

She pointed to a huge cake that stood right in the centre of the display.

"*Yeah!*" Joe grinned. Then he caught Lucy's eye. "Yes, please."

"Coming right up." Mrs Rafferty bustled away.

Lucy was frowning.

"What's up?" Joe asked. "It's great here. It's everything you said it was!" He paused. "Lucy? What is it?"

"Oh…" Lucy came round. "It's nothing. It's just…"

She looked at the big chocolate cake, from which Mrs Rafferty was cutting a slice for Joe.

"I don't remember imagining that."

"Why are there no other children here?" Joe asked, after tea. They were walking back along the promenade.

"What?" Lucy asked.

"Well," Joe peered around. A man in a white bowler hat was selling ice creams. Down on the beach, an elderly man had thrown a tennis ball, and his dog was gambolling for it excitedly amidst the gently lapping waves. "There's all kinds of people here. But no kids."

"I don't want them here," Lucy said shortly. "Other children are stupid. They wouldn't understand."

She led Joe to the steps down to the beach.

"Come on. There's someone I want you to meet."

They walked down the steps and along the shore. Close to the water's edge was a tall, metal structure – a seat at the top of a long ladder.

"Hang on." Joe looked at the calm waters, empty except for the dog that was running for its ball for the umpteenth time. "Why d'you need a lifeguard? Don't look like anyone's gonna be in danger."

"It's my world," Lucy said, again. "I can have a lifeguard if I want one."

She paused by the ladder, and looked upwards.

"Hi, Cody!" she called.

Joe looked up. There had been no one sitting on the metal seat a moment before, he was sure of that.

But there was now.

A tall, athletic young man came scrambling down the ladder and stood, smiling, before Lucy. He was suntanned, very good-looking, with fair hair and startlingly blue eyes.

"Hi, Lucy."

Joe recognised the twanging accent as Australian. The young man gave them an attractive smile.

"Hi, Cody," Lucy said, a little bashfully. "This is my cousin Joe."

"How are you, Joe?" Cody nodded to Joe.

"Cody's over here from Australia," Lucy explained, unnecessarily. "He makes sure we're all safe. Down here on the beach."

"For my sins." Cody grinned.

Having said this, he stopped and stood stock still. It was as if he were waiting to be told what to say next.

"An Australian lifeguard?" Joe muttered to Lucy. "On an English beach?" He looked puzzled. "I've seen him… doesn't he look a bit like… you know? That actor. In that soap…?"

"No," said Lucy sharply. "He doesn't."

She turned, dreamily, back to Cody.

"He's Cody. And that's all that matters."

Joe shrugged. He took a step away from Lucy.

Bored, he reached into his pocket to find something to do. He found a spare chocolate wrapper from Lucy's selection box… 50p Grandad had given him on Boxing Day… an action figure.

He played with the action figure for a moment. It

was the usual sort of figure… a tough-looking muscular man in futuristic gear, his eyes invisible behind mirrored shades. The laser gun he was holding was coming off his outstretched hand… Joe adjusted it…

The next moment, there was a shriek of power, and a deafening explosion.

Cody yelled, and Lucy gave a scream, as a laser beam appeared from nowhere and hit the lifeguard's tower in a shower of sparks.

"Cody!" Lucy yelled. She ran to Cody, who was rubbing his arm painfully where the sparks had caught it. "Are you OK?"

"Yeah." Cody grimaced. "I think so…"

Slowly, all three of them turned to see where the beam had come from.

Their eyes widened.

Joe's action figure stood before them, full-size, a real person, its gun pointed at them.

Abruptly, it turned and set off at a brisk jog up the beach.

The next moment, it was out of sight.

"What – !" Lucy turned to Joe.

Joe took a step back. Lucy's expression was quite terrifying.

"*What – did – you – do?*"

"It was…" Joe tried to sound nonchalant. "It was just – my action figure… he's, like… this cartoon…"

"What did I say to you?" Lucy hissed. "What did I tell you? This is *my world*! We only have to believe in something here, and it happens. And you bring in -"

She stopped. She stared out to sea.

A moment before, the sky had been cloudless, the sea calm.

Now, black clouds had appeared. Closing in across the horizon. And the sea was looking rough and unsettled.

The dog that had been fetching the ball came running back to its master, yapping, yowling, afraid.

"Lucy." Cody sounded just as afraid himself, despite being the biggest and strongest of the three of them. "What's going on?"

"I don't know." Lucy's brow had clouded along with the sky. "We need to find out. Now."

She turned, tenderly, to the injured Cody.

"Get Mrs Parkhouse the District Nurse to take a look at your arm," she told him. "I'll send her along as soon as I can."

She grabbed Joe by the arm. Joe found himself heading for the steps back to the promenade.

"There's only one person who'll know what's going on. And…"

She glared suddenly, and Joe shrank back from her gaze.

"If there is something wrong. I'll know who to blame."

Lucy led Joe away from the promenade, uphill towards the houses stacked above the town. The sky looked really nasty and stormy now, and a cold wind was starting to blow.

They passed by some ornamental gardens, and paused.

There had obviously once been a magnificent display of flowers.

But now the flowers were dead, withered and charred.

Lucy was looking angrier by the moment. She turned away from Joe and ran towards a row of old red-brick houses that lay to their right.

When she spoke again, it was not to address Joe. She seemed, more than anything, to be speaking to herself.

"There has to be a way. He must know. *We – can't – let – this – happen. Not – to – my – lovely – world.*"

Joe found himself running to keep up with her.

"Lucy," he panted. "Where are we going?"

"There's only one man who'll know," Lucy answered grimly. "One man in town. The first character I ever thought of. The oldest – and the wisest."

They entered the front garden of one of the red-brick houses.

Standing near the front window, dressed in a checked shirt, corduroy trousers and a battered straw hat, a tall man stood carefully tending his roses. He had grey hair and a weather-beaten complexion, and looked totally relaxed as he carried out his work.

"Victor!" Lucy ran up to him.

"Lucy." The man smiled gently. He didn't sound at all surprised to see Lucy and Joe dashing into his garden. He pointed upwards to the darkening sky. "I think I know why you're here."

"Out there -" Lucy gasped. "With a laser gun. A man is – it was Joe's -"

Joe looked into the gentle face of the man called Victor. There were so many lines… a real maze… but all leading back to a pair of very kind brown eyes… it looked like the face of someone who always understood.

"I heard about him," Victor said in his deep, thoughtful voice. "People keep coming by. Telling me. Chaos and destruction all over town. He's destroyed houses. Shops. The Arboretum…"

"Oh no!" Lucy howled.

"And your statue," said Victor.

Lucy blinked, almost in tears.

"The townspeople put that up to me!"

"Yes…" said Victor softly. "Yes… of course we did."

Lucy looked up to the sky, the gathering storm.

"And this?"

"I always knew it would come." Victor suddenly seemed very busy with his roses. "There was always going to be a storm. Had to be. Something had to bring chaos. The only thing was – what? Now, we know." He made a careful movement with the secateurs he held. "Strange how things turn out."

There was silence, finally broken by Lucy.

"What can we do?"

"Await the storm." Victor put the secateurs down, and reached for a watering can. "See what follows.

What else can any of us do?"

He turned and looked straight into Lucy's eyes.

"I should get under cover if I were you."

Lucy hesitated a moment. Then her face set in a determined look.

"No."

She grabbed Joe's hand and led him away. She didn't bother to say goodbye to Victor.

Victor shrugged. He returned to his work.

When he spoke again, it was to himself.

"Young folk… Always asking questions. But they never want to take advice."

He dead-headed one of the roses expertly.

"Never want to take advice."

Lucy and Joe were halfway back down the street when the storm began.

There was a blinding flash of lightning, a thunderclap that seemed to tear the whole of Sandyways in two.

Then the rain came. Buckets of it. In no time, Lucy and Joe were drenched.

Everywhere, people were yelling, screaming, running to find shelter. They were the reactions of people who'd never seen a storm before.

"No!" Lucy was shouting, above the commotion. "Keep calm, everyone! You know we've faced worse than this before. Everyone -"

No one was listening. Everyone was running for cover.

"Lucy!" Joe cried. "What's happening!"

"What's happening?" Lucy snapped. "You heard Victor! Chaos is happening! Destruction is happening! My lovely world's coming to an end! And it's all because of *you*."

She rounded on Joe.

"*You* did this, you stupid little boy! *You* made this happen!"

She grabbed Joe by the upper arms.

"Lucy." Joe blinked. Rain trickled down his forehead, and his eyes were wide and afraid. "Let go of me."

Lucy didn't. She placed her face right up to Joe's.

"*You* did this! *You* destroyed all I've worked for!"

Her voice rose to a scream.

"Maybe it would be better if my world survived and *you just didn't exist!*"

The next moment, her hands dropped to her sides.

Joe had gone.

"No…" Wildly, Lucy looked from left to right.

There was no sign of the little boy.

"No!" Lucy cried. "Joe! Joe! I didn't mean -"

A moment later, water was running down her face.

But this time, it wasn't rain.

Alone, wet and miserable, Lucy ran back along the promenade.

It was so dark now, and the cold wind was rising to a gale. And a sort of mist was closing in from the tempestuous sea. Lucy could hardly see where she was going.

She made for the first point of shelter – Mrs Rafferty's.

Inside, the tea room was deserted. Rain and wind battered against the windows, and what had once been a warm log fire was now a pile of cold ashes.

Lucy sank exhausted into a chair, at the table she had shared with Joe.

Then she cried, more and more and more tears, until not a millimetre of her face was dry, until she had no energy left to weep any more.

When the tears finally cleared, she just sat there dumbly, looking at the empty chair where her cousin had sat.

She didn't know how long she stayed like that. But all she remembered afterwards was looking up, and seeing Mrs Rafferty there.

"Lucy."

Lucy made no reply.

"Sorry to disturb you, dear." Mrs Rafferty sounded as gentle and unconcerned as ever. "But I've had a message for you."

"What?" Lucy raised her weary head from the table to look at Mrs Rafferty.

"Well… of sorts." Mrs Rafferty held out a cup and saucer. "It was in the tea leaves. Odd for them to be so clear. But it said: *In the flames.*"

In the flames?

Lucy turned towards the log fire.

It was lit again, and burned brightly.

"Why not take a look?" Mrs Rafferty sounded almost mischievous. "Looks like someone's trying to get in touch with you."

With that, she slipped away, disappearing back towards the kitchen.

Slowly, Lucy rose and crossed to the fire. She knelt carefully on the worn old rug, and stared into the flames.

Lucy.

Lucy jumped.

Lucy. You there?

No one had spoken. At least, not out loud. But someone was talking to Lucy, all the same.

The voice seemed to be inside her head.

"Who's that?" Lucy found voice to reply.

Who d'you think? the voice asked, grinningly.

Lucy's eyes widened.

"Joe?"

She stared harder into the fire.

"Where are you?"

Never mind that! Joe's voice insisted. *I'll tell you later. Hey, this is fun!*

"What is?" Lucy shook her head.

Get ready! Joe told her. *I'm coming to save you! There's just one thing. You need to get to the Castle. We might need somewhere to land!*

Land…?

Lucy ran. Along the promenade, towards the Castle. The rain was still lashing down, and the thunder crashed. She was soaked, and more afraid than she had ever been in her life before, but still she ran, following Joe's instructions.

She reached the steps that led to the battlements. Up and up she went, stumbling, panting for breath, right up to the very top.

That's great!

Lucy jumped as the voice returned to her mind.

Now just wait there! the voice told her. *And look up!*

Lucy turned her head away from the lashing waves, up towards the stormy sky.

And when she saw what she saw, she nearly fainted.

With a roar of power, out of the sky came a vast spaceship. A huge saucer-like craft, around the rim of which hundreds of lights flashed in red and green.

There was a rushing of wind to rival that of the storm as the craft appeared directly overhead.

How about that? the voice asked. *This is what I call a story! Now hold on! We're going to teleport you up!*

Lucy held on.

A moment later, a dazzling yellow light shone down on her.

And Lucy disappeared.

"Hi, Lucy."

Lucy blinked.

Still wet and bedraggled, she stood up from the metal floor on which she found herself.

She was standing on the bridge of the spacecraft. A vast control room, straight out of a comic book.

Computer screens flickered. Lights blinked. There were huge red levers and glimmering dials.

At the controls, steering the ship, were two aliens. Huge purple creatures, with eight legs, three hands, two heads and four mouths. They looked like a cross between tarantulas and gigantic plums.

And sitting between them, in the command chair, was Joe.

The storm didn't seem to have affected him. He was dry, and neat – for him – and was grinning. He looked to be having the time of his young life.

"How about that, then?" Joe asked triumphantly. "Hey, you're not the only one with an imagination, you know."

He smiled.

"It was your space portal gave me the idea."

He turned to one of the aliens.

"Hover over the town."

The alien operated controls.

"I'll be in the viewing gallery." Joe hopped up from his chair. He beckoned to Lucy. "Come over here."

Soaking wet, bewildered, Lucy followed Joe up to a platform, where vast windows gave a panoramic view over the town below.

She recognised the street over which they were hovering. It was Victor's.

An extraordinary sight met her eyes.

Joe's action figure stood in the centre of the street. Surrounding it were a dozen of the townspeople. Lucy recognised them all. There was Mr Allendale, the postman. Mrs Denver from the library. There was Mrs Rafferty, her shawl flapping in the breeze. There was Cody. And there was Victor.

None of them was armed. The action figure had its gun. But it was suddenly looking afraid.

Slowly, the townsfolk advanced on the action figure. As they closed in, it backed away, lowering its gun, shrinking, becoming smaller and smaller…

Lucy blinked down at the crowd below.

No one was wet. And no one seemed to be in danger any more. The sky was growing lighter.

The storm seemed to be passing.

Joe smiled. He strode back to the bridge and returned to his command chair. He addressed the aliens.

"Activate time travel function. Take us forward. To when the storm's gone."

"Activating time travel function like, now." One of the aliens pulled a lever.

Joe gripped the arms of his chair.

The ship began to shake.

"Hold tight!"

Lucy blinked.

She was dry. And comfortable. And she felt calm.

A pale sun shone down from a blue sky.

She was standing with Joe on the promenade.

The man in the bowler hat was still selling ice creams.

"Pistachio for you, isn't it, Lucy?" Dressed in an old cotton jacket along with his straw hat, Victor turned from the stall, holding three cornets. "And raspberry surprise for Joe." He held one of the cornets out to Lucy.

Dumbly, Lucy took the ice cream.

She looked around. The promenade was just as before. Yet… She looked more closely.

A few things were different. There were a few bits of litter, crisp packets and waste paper. The buildings were no longer quite so brightly-painted, just a little shabbier. Someone a short distance away was playing a radio.

And there were children. Other children. Running along the beach. Kicking footballs. Shouting and laughing.

Sandyways no longer looked quite so perfect.

But Joe and Victor looked happy enough.

"You see, Lucy," Victor explained. They were walking along the promenade, eating their ices. "You came up with this place, and with me, and with all of us. And everything was good."

He frowned.

"Too good. We didn't know real life. Because nothing ever really went wrong, do you see?"

Lucy was silent. Victor smiled.

"Remember when the invaders came, couple of years ago? You led the counter-attack, and saved us all. But no one would have known what to do, without you. Even you nearly didn't save us, that night. Everybody nearly died."

He took a bite from his cornet.

"Mm. Anyway. I always knew something would have to happen, to change things. If we were going to survive in Sandyways. A storm had to break. We had to have a crisis. And we had to deal with it ourselves. Defeat our own enemies. We had to learn to use our own imaginations. Starting with me."

Lucy remembered something. She took a glance back towards Mrs Rafferty's.

Victor grinned.

"Yes, okay. I am quite fond of chocolate cake."

He looked thoughtfully out to sea.

"It's no longer a world quite so perfect. Nor even quite so yours. But it's better. We're stronger now. We've seen bad things. And by using our imaginations, we've dealt with them."

He paused.

"But to cause the storm... something bad had to come into the world. We were trapped in being perfect. We needed a trigger. We needed someone to come in and cause a bit of chaos."

Carefully, he took the plastic action figure from his pocket and returned it to Joe.

He and Joe exchanged a conspiratorial grin.

"Oh!" Lucy was laughing now. "He's certainly good at that!"

She moved over to Joe and put her arm around his shoulders.

Contentedly, they continued to walk and eat, as the sun shone down from the summer sky.

"*... as the sun shone down...*" Joe finished scrawling on the page, "*from the summer sky.*"

He blinked.

"Thanks for letting me write a bit. I enjoyed that."

"Your writing is terrible," Lucy told him. She picked up another page from the desk. "And that's not how you spell "spaceship"."

She paused.

"Thanks for writing me out of a hole."

Abruptly, she picked up the pages and started to sort them into yet another file.

"What are you doing?" Joe asked.

"I think…" Lucy frowned. "Maybe I've spent too much time in Sandyways. Maybe my real world's here… I think I'll leave it for a bit."

"No way!" Joe protested. "You haven't seen the best bit yet!"

There was a silence, during which Lucy looked sternly at Joe.

He was looking at his most mischievous.

"Joe. What have you done?"

"Happy Christmas!"

There were massive shouts from downstairs.

Lucy and Joe ran out of the room onto the landing and they peered over the banister rail.

Lucy stared at what she saw.

In the hall below were Grandad, and Joe's Mum and Dad – Auntie Brenda, and Uncle Geoff. They looked bright, and cheerful.

And carried armfuls of presents.

Lucy strained to see. She could just make out the calendar on the desk in the hall. It said:

December 25th.

She turned to look at her cousin.

"Joe!"

"Well!" Joe giggled. "We were doing time travel. So I thought – why not? We're going to have Christmas all over again."

"But!" Lucy blinked. "You can't!"

"I'm telling this story," Joe reminded her. "I can do anything I like. Now come on. I'm looking forward to opening my presents again. I'm hoping the socks won't be there, this time. And I reckon I can eat some more turkey."

He looked down.

"Hey, I'm meant to be down there. Arriving. I'd best go down."

He ran for the stairs.

"Joe!" Lucy ran after him. "Hey! You shouldn't mess with – oh! You are totally irresponsible!"

She followed him down the stairs.

"There'd better not be two of you!"

Far away, in his home in Sandyways, Victor built up his fire against the gathering cold. There were Christmas cards on the mantelpiece and holly around the pictures above.

He sat in his armchair and held out his hands contentedly towards the flames.

He paused, as a young voice spoke in his head.

Happy Christmas, Victor.

And Victor raised his glass smilingly in a toast.

Enjoyed this? Why not read…

THE ALIEN IN THE GARAGE AND OTHER STORIES
ROB KEELEY

Neil's little brother is driving him mad. There can't really be an alien living in the garage… can there?

Luke is bored. Adam has too much to do. Until they decide to swap lives…

A camping trip takes a spooky turn when a ghost story seems to be coming true…

These are just some of the tales in this funny and sometimes scary collection. You can also find out whether Liam and Justin would eat earwigs, why aliens like custard creams, and what exactly is the sinister creature lurking outside the tent…

The Alien in the Garage and Other Stories will appeal to boys and girls aged 8-12… And parents reading the stories to their children! Written for those with a boundless imagination, a strong sense of humour and a desire to learn more about their world.

Available now from Matador in paperback and eBook